Everything Happens for a Reason

Kavita Daswani was born in Hong Kong to parents who had emigrated from India. She left school before taking her A-levels and began working as a freelance journalist. She lived in Paris and London before returning to Hong Kong, where she became fashion editor of the *South China Morning Post*. She was also a fashion contributor to CNN International and CNBC Asia. Kavita Daswani now lives just outside Los Angeles with her husband and young son. *Everything Happens for a Reason* is her second novel.

Also by Kavita Daswani

For Matrimonial Purposes

Everything Happens for a Reason

KAVITA DASWANI

HarperCollins *Publishers* India
a joint venture with

New Delhi

HarperCollins *Publishers* India
a joint venture with
The India Today Group
by arrangement with
HarperCollins *Publishers* Limited

First published in UK in 2004 by
HarperCollins *Publishers* Limited

First published in India in 2004 by
HarperCollins *Publishers* India

Third impression 2005

HarperCollins *Publishers*
1A Hamilton House, Connaught Place, New Delhi 110 001, India
77-85 Fulham Palace Road, London W6 8JB, United Kingdom
Hazelton Lanes, 55 Avenue Road, Suite 2900, Toronto, Ontario M5R 3L2
and 1995 Markham Road, Scarborough, Ontario M1B 5M8, Canada
25 Ryde Road, Pymble, Sydney, NSW 2073, Australia
31 View Road, Glenfield, Auckland 10, New Zealand
10 East 53rd Street, New York NY 10022, USA

Printed and bound at
Thomson Press (India) Ltd.

To the family I was blessed to be born into,
and the family I was privileged to marry.

All my gratitude to my agent, Jodie Rhodes, who gave me something every novelist needs: a gem of an idea. And to my editor, Susan Watt, and all the wonderful people at HarperCollins, for their enduring faith in me. Every author should be this lucky.

1

No woman in my family has ever had a job.

No other female in my entire extended clan, as far back as I know, has ever leafed through 'wanted' ads and shuffled nervously in a seat while a stranger asked her about 'job history'. What would she say? That her primary profession was to serve her father and brothers in early life, and her husband and sons later?

So I was completely taken aback when my mother-in-law prodded my stomach with a wooden spoon, complained that I was yet to make her a grandmother, and then insisted that I may as well be of some use and join the workforce.

'America is expensive,' she said, poking the utensil with such vigour that it was a rather good thing there *wasn't* a baby in there. 'This is not India. In this country everybody works.'

It didn't matter that I was a newlywed, in the first flush of marriage, still unpacking the silk saris and silver goblets that had been part of my small but respectable trousseau. It didn't matter that I was still getting acclimatized – not just to living in a strange country, with a man I didn't really know, but also with his parents and his younger sister. And nor did it matter that, as far as I saw it, my most important role in this family was as housekeeper, cook and general errand-runner, duties that came along with my new position as wife and daughter-in-law.

All this, I had expected.

But I had never thought that somebody – least of all a ferocious guardian of tradition like my mother-in-law – would be telling me to go out and look for a job.

In generations of women in my family, I was going to be the first.

It should have made me feel like a trailblazer, a pioneer, a valiant example of a woman's right to be independent.

Instead, the idea terrified me.

Whether by design or circumstance, my parents had never shown my sisters and me much of the world. To them, there was enough to see and do in India without us having to explore what lay beyond the borders of my homeland. It is the same limited vision, I suppose, that I soon realized many Americans have of their own country.

So getting off that plane two months ago at the Tom Bradley Terminal of Los Angeles International Airport, on a muggy day, was a shock in itself. I had stifled the instinct to wail all the way on the flight over, longing to be with my family again although I had just said goodbye to them. I had drifted in and out of restless sleep as watery images of my wedding, just days earlier, seeped through my subconscious. I was trapped in a middle seat on a packed aeroplane, my husband using my armrest on one side, and a large, be-turbaned Sikh doing the same on the other. I hadn't even landed, yet already felt overwhelmed, squashed and small.

When we finally made it out to the airport, I was astonished by not just the huge *numbers* of people, but their different *types*. Television in India doesn't show you the variety of humanity, their complexions and clothes and cultures so removed from my own: the black woman with her tight trousers and inch-long purple nails, checking my immigration papers; the waiflike Chinese man with the small, serious spectacles, waiting for his grey-haired mother to make her way through customs; the fat white fellow bellowing at his children to get out of the way so he could heave his luggage onto a wayward trolley.

The airport already was a world I had never seen, a microcosm of a universe that I knew I would always be apart from, never a part of.

A week after our Delhi wedding, Sanjay and I had arrived in Los Angeles, his home for the past two decades. For the following two weeks, it was going to be just him and me. My in-laws and Sanjay's sister, Malini, had remained in India, travelling and visiting relatives, and presumably looking for a husband for my sister-in-law, who had just turned twenty.

'Welcome.' Sanjay shut the front door behind us. 'This is your new home,' he announced, like the *fait accompli* it was.

The house was located in a quiet street in Northridge, in an area popularly called 'the Valley', which sounds quaint and rural, but in fact is vast and sprawling, and stretches well across the state. Sanjay dropped the bags on the carpet, and moved towards the couch as I stood and looked around.

At least it was a nice home, and for this I could be grateful. One of my friends from Delhi had had an arranged marriage with a man in Chicago, and had arrived there with all the blushing and naïve enthusiasm of a new bride to discover that he was living in a garage.

But here there was plenty of space: a large sitting room, which looked as if it was never used, filled with bulky furniture, marble-topped tables, and a shiny crystal chandelier hanging overhead. A separate dining room boasted a long table, high-backed wooden chairs and a glass-covered cabinet holding glimmering little figurines. In India, this house would be considered a palace, and I very fortunate to live in it.

'Come, I'll show you my bedroom – oh, er, sorry, *our* bedroom,' Sanjay offered, leading me in by the hand.

It was the room of a young man who had yet to

completely shed the remnants of his boyhood: a mess of clothes and newspapers lay strewn across the floor, a big-screen television sat in one corner and remote controls for various other pieces of entertainment equipment were scattered on the bedside table.

'Great, isn't it?' Sanjay grinned.

'It's quite messy,' I said to him, looking around.

'Hah, why would I clean up after myself when my wife, my new *biwi*, will be here to do it for me?' he said, smiling.

'I am *not* your maid!' I shouted, realizing as I was doing so that I had never raised my voice at him before. I knew I should revert to the meek and mild Hindu wife that I had been for the past week, but I was exhausted. 'Don't think that I am some kind of a village bride because I am from India and you are living in America,' I said testily.

Sanjay jumped back, startled, fear in his face.

'I was just joking,' he said. 'Why so mad?'

I walked into the den and pushed a stack of newspapers off the couch so they tumbled to the floor. Sitting down, I began to weep. My ears were still sealed from our descent, my lips chapped from the cold aeroplane air. I was wondering what my family was doing that very second back home: if my father had yet had his morning *chai*, if my mother was scolding the *dhobi* for ruining yet another of her outfits, if Radha was combing her long hair, and Roma tending to the household, and Ria reclining against her bed, her face in a book. I knew that, barring any unforeseen calamity or cause for celebration, I could anticipate only an annual return to India. Other people live forty minutes or three hours away from their parents. Mine were a whole year away.

Sanjay approached me cautiously, and sat on the couch.

'Why are you crying, Priya? I was just joking.'

'I'm sorry,' I said. 'These tears aren't for that. I miss my family. I'm supposed to see your parents as mine, but I don't. This doesn't feel like my home. What if this is a mistake, and we can't get out of it? Then what?' I turned my back to him, and continued to cry.

I felt a murmur of a hand on my back, a gentle stroking of my hair. I could hear him breathing, steadily, tentatively, as if he were not sure if or where to touch me next.

'*Roh-na*,' he said gently, asking me again not to cry. 'We are both new to this. We will make it.'

Looking back, I believe that that was the precise second that my married life began.

Until the start of my new life in America, I had never experienced jet lag. It was, to me, a concept as foreign as seasickness and being hung over, all of which only sophisticated people ever talked about. My first collision with jet lag made me believe that there is something to be said for being confined to the same time zone for all one's life. I couldn't wait for evening to come so

I could finally sleep, but what seemed like an eternal night ended abruptly, hours before dawn. It was when I felt most vulnerable, most alone, still subtly shocked at the sudden transformation of my life.

But when Sanjay and I were awake and alert, he said that showing me around helped him to see old things as new again, that he loved the look on my face as I marvelled at the cut-price offers on batteries and baby lotion at the 99-Cents shop, and the warehouse stores – which were the size of Bihar, I thought – where people bought twelve-packs of pizza. American supermarkets were the stuff of legend in India, sightseeing venues in themselves. To me, it was like wandering through a giant lit-up refrigerator. Apple sauce, which doesn't even exist in Delhi, here took up an entire lane. Even half these bottles wouldn't fit into Jagdish's, the dried goods store near my old home where the servants buy sacks of rice and *dals* and packets of stiff Indian-made chewing gum.

On my first visit to our neighbourhood supermarket, the day after we arrived in America, I shuffled down the aisle, pulling my sweater tightly around me as I approached the frozen foods section, with its big, frosty bins in the centre. I reached in and pulled out boxes of ice cream and pies, chicken and gravy, peas and potatoes and corn, incredulous that all that food could come out of a small square of cardboard and that there was no chopping or dicing involved.

'Discounts, special offers, extra savings,' said the cashier as I paid. 'Just fill in this form, and join our club.' I smiled with pride as I signed the application, impatient to call my parents and tell them that I was, so soon into my life here, a member of something.

At home that evening, Sanjay showed me how to make tofu burgers and fruit smoothies. He spent three hours filling my head with so many DVD-CD-TV-VCR-laptop-desktop instructions that, by the end, I was dizzy. He showed me where all the light switches were and how to open the garage door and what to do if the alarm system went off. He demonstrated the function of the waste-disposal system, and seemed baffled that I had never seen one before.

'Don't you have garbage disposals in India?' he asked.

'Yes,' I answered. 'It's called the street.'

But I remained perplexed, scared to touch anything for fear that it would cause the house to collapse or the kitchen to explode. I asked Sanjay where the torches were, and he had no idea what I was talking about until I described them.

'In America, they are called flashlights,' he said. 'What do you need one for?'

'For the blackouts.'

'That's what happens when you have too much to drink. Here, we call them power outages. And they almost never happen. You keep forgetting, you are not in India any more,' he said to me gently, laughing.

When Sanjay went off to work the following day, I began my role as wife in earnest. I started to unpack my personal belongings, all the accumulations and acquisitions of almost a quarter-century of living, pared down to two suitcases. Sanjay had cleared out a small section of his wardrobe, which was barely enough for the contents of my trousseau. It had stretched my parents, but they had given me six each of evening ensembles, saris, and daytime outfits – the wealthiest Delhi brides got upwards of twenty each, while the poor were lucky if they received two. I somehow had to find space for all this in a sliver of cupboard no wider than my own person. When Sanjay had showed me proudly how much room he had made for me, I had asked him meekly if perhaps he could afford a little more, but he showed me his dozens of knitted sweaters and suits and bulky winter jackets, and told me that, for now, I would have to make do.

By the time my in-laws returned, it was up to me to see to it that the house sparkled like marble in the moonlight. As is the custom for a bride, my trousseau consisted almost entirely of new clothes, but I had thankfully thought to pack two old outfits for days such as these, 'heavy cleaning days'. I shrugged into a pale green salwar kameez, a traditional tunic top and flared trousers, which was flecked with old corn oil and turmeric stains that the *dhobi* wasn't able to remove.

Comfortably clad, I moved sofas and cleaned underneath. I placed a ladder in front of the wall unit, and wiped on top. I scrubbed toilets and vacuumed carpets and threw out old newspapers. I even mopped down the dusty floors in the garage, astonished all the while that with two women living here, the house had been allowed to get this dirty. It was almost as if they were waiting for me to arrive.

The last room left to clean was that of my sister-in-law, Malini. At the *sagri* ceremony before the wedding, when the family of the groom celebrates and welcomes the arrival of a bride, she had garlanded me and placed a kiss on my cheek, and seemed almost to mean it. I remembered looking down and catching a glint of something on her stomach. For a moment, I thought that perhaps a chunk of glitter had fallen from my hair onto her belly, but upon closer inspection saw that Malini had a ring pierced through her navel. As she caught me staring, my eyes agog, she covered herself with her sari, and quickly moved away.

So I was sure that Malini would hate knowing that I had been in her room, and I had to confess that it was more my curiosity than any slovenliness on her part that drove me in here. I looked around and wondered what it must have been like to have grown up here, in America. The room was dark, with thick yellow curtains blocking out the sunlight. A slim bed rested against a wall, with a matching dressing table and bedside cabinet next to it. Furry teddy bears and monkeys spilled over the light orange flowered eiderdown, and a stack of *Teen People* magazines lay neatly on a side table. On the dressing table were photos in frames – Malini with Sanjay or with her parents, another as a lone Indian girl in a group of Americans. I didn't remember her being this pretty. Her hair was cut short and smooth in a modern style, her teeth white and shiny, no doubt using one of the three thousand types of toothpaste you can find in America. In all the pictures, she was wearing jeans and a short shirt – pink in one, white in another, floral in one after that. I knew I shouldn't, but I felt compelled to open her wardrobe and look through it: there were jeans and cute tops and small jackets, the kind of smart clothes that I had seen people in the supermarket and on the streets wear.

Later in the week, as I took out another load of trash, the postman was stuffing mail into the box outside. I had seen him from the window, but this was the first time I was standing so close to him.

'Hey, how's it going?' he asked. 'How many days a week do you work here?'

'Pardon me?'

'I didn't know that the Sohnis had hired a maid. Good idea – they seem so busy. How often do you come?'

'I'm not the maid,' I replied quietly. 'I'm the wife.'

2

Within days of arriving here, I knew what Sanjay meant when he talked about America and its 'bumper-sticker mentality'.

'See,' he said, pointing out certain vehicles on the streets as we made our way to the DMV, the Department of Motor Vehicles, so I could apply for a driver's licence. 'Here, everybody wants to tell everyone everything. Even the cars have something to say.' In twenty minutes, I counted fifteen such displays of personal information brandished on the back bumpers of vehicles – someone boasting of a child's academic achievements at school, their pride at being an American, or, alternatively, exhorting everyone to 'Give Peace a Chance'. People lumbered by alone in huge cars that blocked roads and took up one-and-a-half parking spaces. They ate and drank and watched TV and talked on tiny phones as they drove what looked like streamlined tanks, their interiors larger than a family of four in India would live in.

People in this country were not shy, and did not expect others to mind their own business. I would queue at the post office, clutching close to my chest envelopes and packets addressed to my family in Delhi, and by the time I was at the counter, I could have penned a thesis on the person in front of me. A typical 'Hey, how are you?' thrown my way would launch a mostly one-sided conversation revealing their last divorce and an argument with their doctor about how to treat a hernia, all while I stood and nodded politely.

At the gym, which Sanjay insisted I join, telling me that everyone in America exercised, modesty was a non-issue. In the changing room, as I slipped into my workout clothes behind the safety of a toilet cubicle, women stood naked as they slathered their legs with moisturizer, or combed the wetness out of their hair, talking with each other about cardio, carbs and calories. They had no body hair except where they should have it, unlike myself and all the other women I grew up with, who went to salons where 'full body waxing' was a standard request. At my jazzercise class, they wore skin-tight shorts and bra tops, while I huffed and puffed in track pants and a thigh-length T-shirt, hiding in the back next to the dark blue mats. Afterwards, I refused even to take a shower there, noticing that the curtain barely covered the width of the shower stand

After Sanjay left for the office every day, to the bag importing business he ran with his father, and once the day's housework was done, I had made a habit of enjoying the solitude of my life. Television became my best friend, as I marvelled at the cleverness of Claire Huxtable and the frothy antics of Lucy Ricardo and the dry sophistication of those Designing Women. This was, I was sure, how the real America lived, with charming coincidences and laughs every second, fascinating people and clever situations round every corner.

Unlike everyone on television, I wasn't ecstatically happy as a newlywed. There was no giggling, romantic haze. But I had never expected that, so my state of modest contentment and growing adjustment seemed perfectly acceptable. My grandmother used to tell my sisters and me that constant, uninterrupted joy was a myth, and fundamentally bad luck.

'The more you laugh, the more you will eventually cry,' she used to say. 'Tragedy always visits people who are too happy.'

It was better, she taught us, that dull, fractious, and even miserable moments are folded into a life of moderate satisfaction.

My grandmother was never wrong.

The rain pelted down thick and hard from the skies like silvery shards of glass. Sanjay had phoned to say he would be working late with a customer, leaving me alone with tea and magazines. On the cover of one was a picture of Jennifer Aniston – I already knew the names of everyone who appeared on those glossy television shows. The actress was staring sexily into the camera, a tiny pair of jeans encasing her slender hips. I knew that she was married to Brad Pitt, who is famous even in India.

I should have been at the gym, but, today anyway, was tired of obeying the fitness instructors as they shouted their orders: 'Activate those inner thighs! Contract those abs! Tighten! Tighten! Recover!' I didn't want to work my 'obliques', whose location in my body escaped me, despite two years of human biology class in school.

Instead, I chose to spend my afternoon reclining on the moss-green leather sofa in the den. Having finished the last of my *chai*, I helped myself to yet another oatmeal raisin cookie from the platter on the low glass table.

There was only the sound of the shower outside, splashing fiercely on the pavement, its defiance keeping me company. Soon, I would have to get dinner started, even if consuming all that sugar had sapped me of energy. Perhaps I would just reheat last night's leftover grilled aubergine, and throw in some boiled potatoes and cumin to lend a different flavour. A tired Hindu bride was nothing if not inventive.

This would be my last day of indulgence. Tomorrow, my in-laws would be coming home, and their demands, I knew, would easily supersede my own. No leftovers would sully my father-in-law's table, and my mother-in-law would not allow me to put my feet up for a second. Malini, I was sure, would have something to say about everything.

So today, I could take my final afternoon nap.

16

So soundly did I sleep, that I didn't even hear Sanjay come in. When I opened my eyes, groggily and unsure, a trace of saliva had dribbled out of my mouth and onto the arm-roll of the couch, where I had been resting my head. I was still embarrassed for Sanjay to see me like this; I locked the bathroom door whenever I was inside, baffled by the practice I'd seen on those cable television shows of so many couples who did everything in front of one another.

'Oh, you're home,' I announced, looking up at him sheepishly. 'I'm so sorry. I must have been really tired. What time is it? I'll get up now, get dinner ready.' My head still spinning and heavy with sleep, I swung my legs off the couch and started to make for the kitchen.

'Don't worry,' Sanjay said, grabbing my arm. 'Forget that. Come, I want to take you out for dinner.'

'But why? It's nobody's birthday.'

'Never mind,' Sanjay replied. 'We'll go out and enjoy ourselves. They're all coming back tomorrow. It's our last evening together like this.'

It was my first look at an American buffet. Before I was married, when friends and relatives had returned from trips to the US, they would almost invariably talk about the food. 'Big big plates,' they would say, recalling the highlights of their trip. 'Big big portions. So much to eat. So easy to become fat.'

Here, on counters that lined the length of the restaurant,

moist yellow kernels of corn sat next to glistening green peas. Slices of blood-red beet were arranged near broccoli shaped like miniature trees. And all those beans – kidney and black-eyed, chickpea and lima.

'And see, this is only one section,' Sanjay said. Holding plastic trays, we walked to an area where large stainless steel vats steamed with soup – minestrone and split pea, clam chowder and chicken noodle. Further down, there were trays of cheese-laden breads and garlic rolls, pizza slices and spongy muffins filled with fruit. Jellies wobbled and white cream on cakes twirled and swirled. After all those cookies at home, I wasn't even hungry, but this seemed too good to pass up.

'So, what did you do today?' Sanjay asked, when we'd sat down and he was slicing into a stack of tomatoes. 'Are you finding that you are getting more settled in?'

I wished, at that moment, that I could have been like the smart lady with the perfect English accent on *Cheers*, who always had something funny to say, or the cheerful red-haired mother on *Happy Days*. Instead, I told Sanjay about someone calling to offer me a credit card, which had been the highlight of my day, but that the offer was revoked when I told her I'd never had one before.

'Actually, I think I'm a little nervous,' I said, revealing something to Sanjay that I had just begun to know myself. 'I'm worried about your family coming tomorrow – if we all will, you know, get along.'

'I understand,' said Sanjay, nodding. 'You'll do fine. They'll grow to love you,' he reassured, squeezing some mustard out of a packet onto a portion of French fries. He raised his earnest face and looked straight into mine. 'You just have to obey them, keep quiet, smile, and everything will be great,' he said.

The spoon of split pea soup I was holding close to my mouth suddenly stopped moving, lingering on the edge of my lips. I had known in principle that this was how good daughters-in-law behaved, but had never thought my husband would be actually giving me instructions.

'What if they tell me to do something and I can't obey them?' I asked him, fearful. 'What if, no matter what I do, they are still never happy with me?'

'My parents are reasonable people,' Sanjay said. 'As long as you don't argue with them, everything will be fine. And there is no need for you to argue with them because, as I say, they are reasonable people. I told you, just stay quiet, and obey. Come, are you finished? Let's go home.'

The next day at the airport I dutifully bowed my head to greet my husband's parents, something I knew they would expect me to do first thing in the morning and last thing at night for at least the first year of married life.

My father-in-law had been trundled over in a wheelchair; usually, he was quite happy with a cane, which he felt he needed after a fall in a slippery bathtub a few years ago (after which, this being America, he sued the builder of the house). But he was never one to reject a free ride, so when it was offered to him by way of a wheelchair, he wasn't about to decline. Malini and I hugged awkwardly, she staring at my daffodil-yellow sari and me at her slim-fitting velvet tracksuit.

We made our way to the car park opposite the terminal, and began unloading the mounds of luggage. Inside those suitcases were dozens of packets of *masala* and *chevda*, the foods that no bonafide Indian home should be without, and all the silks and brocades that my in-laws had accumulated in Delhi, as part of my dowry and on their own.

I helped my father-in-law into the front passenger seat, and my mother-in-law into the back. Malini got in on the other side. Sanjay was revving up the engine as I squeezed the last little sack into the boot, and slammed the lid down. As soon as I did so, Sanjay, thinking everyone was in, drove off, leaving me standing there. He was the only one who realized I was missing, just as he was turning the corner, and came back to fetch me.

'Sorry, my mistake,' he said, as I opened the door and got in, my mother-in-law looking displeased as she made room for me.

At home, I carted the luggage off into the bedrooms, rubbed my mother-in-law's feet, and began reheating dinner – which had been ready since eight this morning.

'You know, Ma, Priya has been working very hard for your arrival,' Sanjay said, as she enjoyed a cup of tea. 'She's been really great. The house is spotless, no? And she's learned to do all the grocery shopping and everything. She knows to buy only generic brands, and she uses coupons and all.'

I smiled, touched by his observation.

'Hah, hah, very good,' my mother-in-law responded. 'What's for dinner?'

I had prepared South Indian cuisine in honour of their arrival. I lay the platters of steamed *idli* and spicy *sambar* on the table, which I had covered with white paper doilies. The bright overhead light shone on the condiments and cutlery, making the table setting look like something that might be photographed in a magazine.

Dinner was over quickly, with none of those lingering conversations I had seen on those daytime movies, the ones where brandies were poured and dainty chocolates devoured. My dreaded first night at home with the in-laws seemed to have gone off OK.

Now, I just had the rest of my life to worry about.

3

It's true when people say marriage is 'hard work'. There are floors to scrub and shelves to dust and mirrors to wipe. There are onions to chop and spices to sizzle and pots of tea to brew. There are a hundred things to do every day, none of which, I soon realized, had anything to do with the actual marriage itself.

At least that was what *my* marriage was like.

I knew, in marrying Sanjay, that I was going to be part of a traditional joint Hindu family, two generations under one roof. My own parents had done it that way back in Delhi, as had everyone I knew. In many Hindu families, for a son to have his own home is somewhere between a scandal and a tragedy. Male children are born to care for their parents, and then they marry and bring a wife into the house. She is expected to be 'homely'. In America, that means 'not good-looking'. In India, it means 'taking care of the home and being there all the time' – with the exception of dashing off to buy peas.

So it wasn't as if I hadn't been prepared for any of this. In India, where labour is cheap, we could say things like: 'I'll send my man to pick you up.' There, you can live well as a member of the middle class. In America, everything always seems to be a struggle, what with terrifying taxes that you can't corrupt your way out of, and car registrations, and electricity bills.

Thankfully, my mother had groomed my sisters and me for what she called a 'domestic life'.

'Darlings, you *have* to learn how to take the entire skin off an apple before it turns brown!' she used to say to us, as we endured potato-peeling and parsley-chopping rituals.

All of which, I have to say, has now come in very handy.

But nobody ever tells you what *really* happens when a marriage begins; when the wedding reception is over and the gifts are cleared and a girl moves in with a boy – and, in my case, his entire family. Nobody prepares you for that. Like a Hollywood ending, you never know what happens after the credits have rolled and it's the morning after the couple have walked off into the sunset.

Like all other girls of my age and background, my view of marriage was shaped by commercials and Indian soap operas, where men never saw their wives looking anything other than flawless. There were no acne breakouts, no runny noses, no belching or burping in marriage. I imagined that my future husband would always be clean, sweet and smiling. I would always have waxed legs and a pristine complexion. We would never have a moment's silence between us. He would garland me with gold chains and I, petite in his oversized pyjama shirt, would kiss his stubbly cheek every morning.

But my marriage, as tender as it could occasionally be, was nothing like that.

It was, in the end, a guy in a vest, scratching himself, and a girl wondering what to make for dinner. For us, there were no trips to Ethan Allen for mahogany book-cases, no putting up pictures together and standing back, arms around one another, looking at the straight and perfect job we had just done. There were no nose-nuzzling nights with a bottle of wine in front of the fire. It was about me being absorbed into the life of Sanjay and his family, without leaving much of myself behind.

Sanjay had promised me that when his family returned from India, they would throw a grand reception to intro-duce me to all their friends. I had already selected the sari I would wear to the party, a cream chiffon one that had been a gift from my meddlesome Aunt Vimla, and the one thing about her I actually liked. I would wear it with the gold I had been given on my wedding day, and I would be poised and pure and everyone in my in-law's Northridge circle of friends would marvel at how Sanjay Sohni had found such a nice wife.

But my mother-in-law told me, a week after their return, that there would be no such party.

'Enough money was spent in India at the wedding,' she said, referring to my father's expenses and some imaginary ones of her own. 'No need to do anything here. *Bas*, you'll slowly meet people. Our friends will have lunches and teas. Then they can see you. Anyhow, you are busy with the house. No time to socialize.'

Sanjay was one of the last in his group to get married, so we instantaneously had a young-couple clan to be a part of. Every few Saturday nights, once I had prepared dinner for my in-laws and cleaned the kitchen, Sanjay took me out with his friends. We went for dinners in loud restaurants where all the boys drank beer and paid me no heed. There was Rajesh and Naresh and Prakash, married to girls named Seema and Dina and Monu, and they looked me up and down, with no attempts made to be subtle about it, each time we met. All the wives worked, and seemed proud of it. When they weren't talking about bad bosses and car payments, they gossiped about other girls. They wore quite smart Western clothes, and seemed to have forgotten the days when they were new to America from India, and had dressed tradition-ally, just like me. They were Indian girls, but American now, and I knew when I met them that they would never become my real friends, because whenever I saw them they made me long to be with my sisters again.

Whenever Sanjay wanted to see these people, I went along with him. When we returned home, I told my in-laws that we had had a nice time, and said nothing as Sanjay lied to them about how much dinner had cost. I set the alarm clock for early the next day so I could get up and make tea. Then I touched their feet, even if they had already gone to bed. Between that and picking up the trail of clothes and other items Sanjay would leave in his wake, I knew I would be spending much of my marriage at a ninety-degree angle.

I was a good Hindu wife. This is just what I *did*. Dutiful, devoted and ever so downtrodden, but always happy and smiling. I was to do what my in-laws said.

And now, I was to go and find a job.

4

Vivacious! was my favourite magazine in the whole world. When it arrived every month at our home in Delhi, I would tear off the Cellophane covering, sit down with a jug of *nimbu pani* and not get up again until I had read the issue cover to cover. There were none of those 'Ten Wicked Ways to Please Your Lover' columns like I was embarrassed to see that American magazines are filled with. Instead, I read features with titles like 'Ghee – Not Just in Your Mother's Kitchen'. There were articles about at-home pedicures (or at least how to train the maids to give them), the importance of yoga in pre-natal care, and how curtains can be made from those unwanted silk saris. Delhi socialites were interviewed about their most memorable parties, and Hindi movie-stars about how *grrreat* their co-stars were in their latest films.

When I was still a single and carefree Delhi girl, I had been priming myself to ask my father if I could apply to *Vivacious!* for a job. I had realized, as I flicked through the crisp pages of the magazine, occasionally holding it up to my nose to smell the new print, that I wanted to write those stories. I had composed plenty of essays for my degree in English literature, for which I almost always got at least a B-plus, so there must have been some ability in me to put words together. My father, I knew, would probably refuse, and repeat to me that 'no woman in this family has ever worked outside the house – and look, your sisters are all at home where they belong', which is something he said to any of us when we brought up the subject. And I had to confess that it was not important enough to get into an argument about. Still, there had been no harm in asking again.

But then marriage happened to me. Literally. This profound life change fell upon me as suddenly and fatefully as buckets of dirty water sometimes tumble from buildings upon Delhi pedestrians, as they walk by drinking coconut juice and eating tamarind-soaked rice crispies.

So the night that my mother-in-law suggested I look for a job, my first thought was to reprise my former ambition of being a journalist. My grandmother used to say to me, 'After marriage, do what you want. Nobody wants a working girl as a bride, but maybe later, if you are lucky, your husband will permit you to have your dreams.'

I had hoped that my in-laws would reward my proven subservience by acquiescing to a small request that *I* had.

'Absolutely not!' my father-in-law shouted when I mentioned it, reacting as if I had told him I wanted to become a stripper. 'I'm not having a daughter-in-law do that kind of nonsense work. Reporter-beporter, hah! This is a small community, and I will not let people say they have seen the wife of my only son with different men, meeting them alone. Maybe you'll have to do interviews in hotel rooms? Maybe they will give you alcohol? Then what will you do? If you were a doctor, something *respectable*, I would not have a problem. But none of this going here and there by yourself. I will not tolerate it. You must find a *simple* job.'

New brides were not supposed to argue with their in-laws, so I deferred to my husband, hoping he would step in. But he said nothing, keeping his eyes on his plate the entire time, playing with a *paratha*.

'Fine, Mummy, Papa,' I said quietly. 'As you wish.'

It was disappointing, but I took comfort in my grandmother's words as she would observe any of life's minute dramas and greater mysteries.

'Things come about the way they are supposed to,' she would often repeat. 'Everything happens for a reason.'

5

Those words wafted around in my head as I sat in my car in front of a gleaming chrome and steel building in Beverly Hills, about to go into my fifth job interview in ten days. The sun was glinting off the mirrored surface of the building with such brightness that the number on the top of the entrance was momentarily hidden, so I couldn't be sure I was even in the right place. It looked, well, too *nice*. I had so far been turned down for salesgirls positions in three stores – the interviewers had each time surveyed my drab, shapeless Indian outfit and told me the position had already been filled. And the owner of the local 7–Eleven rejected my application because I had 'no experience', even though I reminded him that I had quite a way with a broom, and was pretty sure I could master the cash register in no time.

Apparently, in this country, having no job before the age of twenty-four isn't the soundest recommendation, and the current flat economy didn't help. Had I been in

India, the only reason I would be out seeking work was because a search for a husband had, for whatever reason, been deferred. There, to be twenty-four and gainfully unemployed was a good thing.

I checked my watch. It was exactly nine o'clock. I was on time, and, as sophisticated as this place looked, it *was* the correct address. I took a deep breath, said the prayer invoking Laxmi, the Goddess of Prosperity, that I always said before one of these, and went in. Hopefully, today, She would listen to me.

'Um, hello, I'm here to interview for the receptionist position,' I said to the security guard in the cool marble foyer, pulling out the newspaper ad. He made a call, and then gave me a 'Visitor' tag, which I plastered on my tunic top. In the elevator, I checked myself in the mirror, smoothed down my waist-length hair, wiped off a bit of lip-gloss that had somehow landed on my chin, and hiked up my drawstring trousers so they no longer puddled around my ankles. The red powder that I wore in my hair parting to signify my status as a newlywed wife was still bright and intact. It always drew stares, and many times gasps of concern from strangers who thought that perhaps my scalp was bleeding. In the concentrated light of the elevator, it looked almost sinister. The pendant of the Hindu goddess Durga around my neck shone under the spotlights. The small heels of my slightly scuffed beige shoes added a bit of height to my frame, and I noticed that I still hadn't regained the weight I'd lost since my wedding, which explained why my trousers – drawstring notwith-standing – couldn't stay up.

When I got out, I saw the words *Hollywood Insider* scrawled in brilliant blue across a set of double glass doors leading to an office. Inside, two girls were sitting on a dark orange sofa in the reception area and on a corner table was a stack of job-application forms. I picked one up and started to fill it out. I had the contents of these almost memorized by now.

The girls, obviously friends, were fashionably dressed and lively, chatting to one another with confidence.

'I'm sure *one* of us will slam-dunk this,' said the first girl. 'I have to admit, things are really looking up for me since I started on the Zoloft.'

'Yeah,' said the other one, chewing gum. 'Can you imagine who we could meet? You know, Colin Farrell could come in through those doors any second.' At that, they both giggled and pretended to swoon, while my only thought was: Colin who?

Sitting behind the reception desk was a woman who looked at least fifteen months pregnant, trying to get comfortable in her chair. I glanced around at the smooth, shiny marble floors, the glass-enclosed offices on either side of me, the huge framed magazine covers featuring famous people that lined the walls. The receptionist, who introduced herself as Dara, asked to speak to each of the other girls first, individually. They conversed quietly while I scribbled my details down on the form. Name: Priya Sohni. Age: 24. Languages: English, Hindi,

Conversational French. I left blank the space next to 'Experience'.

Before I knew it, it was my turn.

'Hi,' Dara said, barely able to move. 'So, as you've probably guessed this is for my position, as I've got more pressing things to do,' she said, pointing to her large, bulbous stomach. 'I'll chat with you first, and then send you off to human resources for a second interview. OK? Right, let's have a look,' she continued, scanning down my form.

'You have all your papers? Legal?' she asked, when she read that my place of birth was India.

'Yes, miss, absolutely,' I replied, nervously winding a handkerchief in and out of my fingers.

'I love your accent,' she said smiling. 'Sounds real nice. So, are you familiar with computers?' she asked, casting a curious glance towards the slim red streak down my hair parting.

'I'm proficient with word processing,' I said.

'Good English, huh?'

'Bachelor's in literature.'

'When do you think you can you start?'

'Um, right away, if you would like,' I replied hopefully.

'That's good to hear,' she said, grimacing and looking down. 'I think my water just broke.'

Five minutes later, as Dara called her husband to come to fetch her, yelling out to me, 'Good luck with the rest of the interview!', I was carted along to the head of human resources, an efficient-looking woman named Hilda. She had short black hair, was dressed in a business suit that seemed a bit heavy for this climate, and asked me to take a seat in her office. I tried not to get my hopes up, but this was the furthest I had ever been.

'You know what the job is, yes?' she asked. 'We're a celebrity magazine. There's lots of answering of phones, taking deliveries, greeting visitors.' As I nodded, she looked at my application from again.

'It says here you're from India. What brought you to America?'

'Marriage. My husband emigrated from India many years ago with his family,' I replied.

She looked up, and put down her pen.

'Was it, an, um, what-do-you-call-them, *arranged* marriage?' she asked, suddenly interested. 'And a joint family? Like on the Discovery channel? Do you all live together?'

'Yes, as a matter of fact we do,' I said, my accent suddenly sounding thick and clumsy in this light-filled room with the modern art on its walls. 'It's quite traditional, how it all happened.' I was conscious of my English, remembering Mrs Pereira from school, who would thwack my palm with a chipped wooden ruler if I slurred words together or dropped letters from their place. Even if I was living in America now, there would never be any 'gonna' or 'wanna' or 'gotta'.

'Yeah, I read something in *Marie-Claire* about brides

moving in with their in-laws,' Hilda continued. 'Hafta say, don't know how you folks do it. It's hard enough living with just my husband, forget his parents.

'I think you've forgotten to fill this in,' she then said, suddenly changing the subject and pointing to the 'Experience' section. My heart sank. This was the part where I was always shown the door.

'I didn't forget,' I said quietly. 'I have not had a job before. This would be my first.'

Hilda looked stunned.

'Not even while you were in college? Not even part time or summers? Well, that's disappointing because the ad did say we needed someone with experience. I'm sorry, I know you came all the way in, but – '

'Please, Miss Hilda,' I stammered, trying not to cry, I couldn't take another rejection, another day of going home empty-handed, and then having to start the search all over again. Already, my in-laws were complaining about how much petrol I was wasting on what they called 'coming up and down', as if it were my fault that nobody wanted to hire me.

'I know I can do the job,' I pleaded to Hilda. 'I learn very quickly and am willing to work hard. Please, just give me a chance.'

Hilda leaned back in her chair. 'You don't want to become an actress, do you?' she asked, narrowing her eyes.

'Oh my, no!' I replied, surprised at the question.

'Then that's about the only thing you have going for you. Everybody else who comes in here thinks that this will be their first step into the industry, as if they'll be discovered by some super-agent as they're sitting behind reception. Like the two girls who were in here before you. I knew they weren't serious. It's infuriating. We fill the position so often that it's become a joke. Dara is the only one we've had that had a legitimate reason for leaving,' Hilda said, shaking her head.

She looked me up and down, clearly not enamoured of my outfit and puzzled by what to her must have looked like a razor slit above my cranium. And I *knew* when I left the house that the waist pouch was a bad idea.

'You're very nice-looking, but you might want to invest in a few new clothes,' she said. 'You're the first person anyone sees when they walk through those doors.'

I nodded eagerly, but was wondering how I was going to get around that one. My in-laws frowned on what they called 'very bad and sexy American-style clothes for cheap girls' – which to them was anything but a baggy sweat-suit. If it were up to them, I would be cruising through Los Angeles in a burkha.

'You're lucky that we need someone to start immediately, and that I can't be bothered to interview any more this morning. So I hope I don't regret this, but I'm going to give you a shot,' she said. 'Welcome to the *Hollywood Insider*.'

Within minutes, I was signing contracts and having my social security card photocopied and being shown around a glossy set of offices by a man called Lou, Hilda's assistant.

'This is where the *Hollywood Insider* is put together. That's just one division of the company, the one you'll be involved with. The rest of the building is ours as well,' Lou said, as if he'd recited the same speech a million times before.

I couldn't help hearing snippets of conversation coming through the glass-enclosed booths, the tops of the cluttered desks filled with flat-screen computers, brightly coloured in-trays, stacks of pens and mobile phones charging. Everywhere there were photographs of movie stars – a big black-and-white shot of Jackie Chan lay on the floor, a signed picture of Julia Roberts was pinned to a corkboard. People were chatting on their phones, scribbling notes, yelling over their desks things like, 'Harrison Ford's guy is on line two.' I was in the same room as people who knew people who knew Harrison Ford, who, like Brad Pitt, was famous even in India.

From what I'd seen in the movies, I had thought I would be sitting in front of a large wall repeating 'Hold, please' every five seconds, switching little wires in and out of sockets. Isn't that what a receptionist did?

Instead, I was installed behind a large circular desk that had a counter above it, making me feel even smaller and more hidden. Jerry, a young man from the IT department, had come along to ask me if I had any questions about how the phone system worked.

'Everyone here has direct lines, so most of their calls come through on those,' he instructed. 'But sometimes people call the main line – that's you – and you'll need to direct them. So here's a list of everyone's names, what their job titles are, and their extensions. And this row of buttons – that's for you if you need to buzz anyone in-house, like my department, or accounting, or security. Especially security,' he said. 'Anyway, you think you got that?'

As soon as Jerry had gone I called Sanjay to tell him that I had got the job, was starting right away, and wouldn't be home until evening.

'Congrats, honey!' he said. He had started calling me 'honey' recently, leading me to believe that he had been watching too much *Days of Our Lives* on the television in his office. 'I've been a bit worried, didn't hear from you all morning,' he said. 'I left a couple of messages on your mobile. As long as everything is OK . . .'

'Yes, fine. Better go now,' I whispered. 'I don't want them to think I'm not doing anything on my first day. I'll speak to you later, hah?'

Hollywood Insider, as I read from a company brochure I found in my desk, was a newcomer to the world of entertainment publishing. Its purpose was to 'provide accurate, entertaining, informative and illuminating news and features on movie stars, their films, and the world

41

they inhabit'. The parent company, Galaxy Holdings, also published a tabloid, called *Weekly Buzz,* which was located two floors down. *Stardom*, the cable television channel Galaxy owned, was an even more recent arrival on the scene.

In between taking and rerouteing calls, I leafed through a few recent issues of the magazine. There were long interviews with major movie stars, short items about production deals gone sour and a page devoted to who was wearing what at last week's premieres. Everyone around me was beautiful and busy, and I gazed at them from behind my desk, where I was barely visible unless I stood up. They were the kind of people that my father, in his infinite cleverness, would describe as 'the impression-making sort'.

In the middle of the morning, a smiling redhead came up to me with a trolley.

'Hi, I'm Deanna from the mail room,' she said. 'You're new here, right? Every few weeks, there seems like there's someone new here. Not that it's a bad job – in fact I think it's a *great* job, but people don't seem to stick around that long. What's your name?' she asked, finally stopping for breath.

'Priya,' I said, standing up. 'Very nice to meet you.'

'Anything to send out?' she asked, scanning the top of the counter above my desk. 'I'll be coming by a few times a day, but this is the first call.'

'Um, nothing yet. Is there anything else I should know?' I asked.

'Well, let's see. For the most part, everyone is super-nice. But,' she said, lowering her voice, 'there's a couple of people down there,' and she motioned with her thumb to the corridor where all the writers sat, 'that can be *really* mean. Just, what's that word, *terrestrial*?'

'I think you mean territorial,' I said.

'Yeah, that, whatever,' she continued, flicking my words away with her hand. 'Some of them down there get *really* snippety about newcomers, think that everyone is after their jobs. I mean, *so* paranoid!' she said, rolling her eyes, and fingering one of the six silver rings that lined her left ear.

'So where you from, anyway?' she asked, cupping her chin in her hand and leaning against the counter on an elbow. 'You got a real unusual accent. What is it, like, Toledo?'

'Um, India, actually,' I said. 'Not Toledo. Delhi.

'Are we allowed to be talking like this?' I asked, looking around nervously. 'I don't want to get caught.'

Deanna looked at me disbelievingly and giggled.

'Where do you think you are – boarding school? It's just an office, for God's sake. Sure we're allowed to talk. It's not like we're in some lock-up, although I guess sometimes it might feel that way!'

Lou came by, and I shuffled some papers, lowered my eyes, and said goodbye to Deanna, who shook her head, rolled her eyes and walked away.

'You can take an hour off for lunch, between one and two,' Lou said. 'Just don't forget to turn the system to

43

voicemail, and check any messages when you get back.'

I was suddenly hungry – I hadn't had any breakfast this morning, convinced I'd be back home in no time – so at exactly one, I made my way back down in the lift, which stopped on each floor until it was filled. I kept my eyes lowered as I heard these people in their relaxed, slurry accents talking about what had happened this morning or debating between Chinese and a sandwich. I was the last to emerge when we reached the lobby, stepped out through the big glass doors, and wasn't sure where to go next. Everyone else had gone off in pairs and groups, leaving me standing there alone. The sun was beating down strong and hard, causing me to squint to find my bearings. Cars whizzed back and forth as I stood in the parking lot, looking out across the wide, busy boulevard. There were dozens of places to eat, and I just had to choose somewhere to go. In a way, it felt lovely to be this free; that the next hour was mine to do with exactly as I wanted, instead of having to cut short my shower, which I often had to do at home, because the aubergine might be burning.

I opened my wallet and found that I still had the twenty dollars that was left over from last week's house-keeping money, which would buy me just about anything, food-wise. A bright yellow awning down the block beckoned me, and I found that it was a little Italian café. I went in, said the radical words 'for one', and was escorted to a small table against a wall. A slim novel was tucked into my handbag – one of my sisters had taught me *never* to leave home without one – and I ordered a dish of vegetable pasta and some water. I was the only person in the restaurant dining alone, and while I recognized some of the other people there from the office, I know that they didn't recognize me. I kept my eyes on my book the whole time, as if raising them and looking around would mean that I was opening myself up to the humiliation, surely, that women feel eating by themselves. And when these people around me laughed, as they did often while in conversation, I was certain that they were laughing at me.

As awkward as I felt, however, this was so much better than standing in the kitchen with my mother-in-law, grinding cumin seeds.

Even if I would still have to do that later.

6

Finally, I knew what people meant when they talked about being in 'commuter hell'. I had been told that once anyone drives in India, getting behind the wheel anywhere else in the world is a dream; Los Angeles, especially, with its infamous freeways, which were never particularly free. There were rules in this country. In Delhi, people parked sideways along narrow streets or in front of entrances or on top of the pavement, safe in the knowledge that it would take two days for a tow truck to get there. Speeding tickets would be torn up with an offer of a few hundred rupees, and it didn't matter if you didn't have your licence on you – or if you didn't have one at all, for that matter. But here, in this land of rules and regulations, I knew that I couldn't just slide by. It had taken me three attempts to get my licence; I kept knocking down those orange cones during the test. And when I was finally a fully qualified member of the driving community, I refused to use those freeways.

'I'm scared to merge,' I said, crying to Sanjay. 'So many cars coming, one after the other, nobody letting me go. I want to stay in one lane only.'

'If you do, you'll end up in Santa Barbara,' he said. 'If you want to live here, you have no choice.' This was why I knew I would never fit in. Other drivers slid in in front of me, whether I was prepared for them or not, and barrelled through lanes as if they owned the roads. I always gave them priority, convinced they had more right to be there than I did. I would rather end up in Santa Barbara than fight for the right exit.

Tonight, after shifting and merging alongside the rest of the cars on the 101 freeway, filled with their stressed-out lone occupants, it wasn't till seven thirty that I finally pulled into the drive of our house.

Our home was distinguished from all the others on the street only by the bunch of dried chilies suspended above the front door, and the small plastic mural of Laxmi embedded into the stucco wall on the right of the entrance.

I opened the door, and saw my family seated around the dining table, about to tuck in.

'Priya, glad you made it home in time. We weren't sure when you would be back. Terrible traffic, right?' said Sanjay, rising from his chair.

My in-laws looked up, while my sister-in-law, Malini waved casually across the room.

'Hiya, *bhabi*,' she said, referring to me in the way that all good girls are meant to call the wives of their elder brothers – although I knew, based on the contents of her closet and the secrets that I sensed lingered in the walls of her bedroom, that Malini wasn't really a good girl.

'We ordered Domino's pizza and garlic bread,' my mother-in-law said, huffily. 'It became late; nothing was ready.'

'Sorry, Ma,' I replied. 'Rush-hour traffic. I think it's going to be like this everyday. I don't know what else to do.'

'Hah, never mind, we'll work something out,' she said, surprisingly sympathetically, cutting stretchy string cheese that connected a slice of pizza to the plate. 'Maybe you just do all the chopping and cutting in the morning before you go, and then Malini and I can fry everything later.'

My sister-in-law, nibbling on a piece of bread, did not look amused.

'You have to learn eventually, *beti*,' my mother-in-law said, addressing her. 'You are twenty now. Soon, we will have to find a boy for you and then what will you do?

'And then,' she continued, turning back to me 'on weekends, we can do everything else – cleaning, dusting, sweeping properly. We will have to make new arrangements because of your job.'

That seemed a pretty equitable arrangement. Besides, didn't everybody in America live this way? Work at work and then come home and work still?

'Anyway, how did everything go?' my father-in-law

asked, his bald spot shining beneath the light, his thick and unruly eyebrows reminding me of a picture I had once seen of the jungles of Borneo. I was surprised by his interest; he usually only interacted with me to tell me that the cauliflower could be crispier.

'Everything went well, Papa,' I replied. 'I think I will like it there.'

'What is your salary?'

I told them, and my in-laws promptly proceeded to work it out in rupees, causing them to *ooh* and *ahh* with delight. It then fell upon Sanjay to remind them that while two hundred thousand rupees was, indeed, a fortune in India, forty thousand American dollars was just forty thousand American dollars, a lot less after tax.

'Better you open a bank account,' my father-in-law advised. 'We will see how much goes towards your own savings, and how much we can use for the house expenses. Also, we have to remember that you won't be working for long. Soon, God willing, baby will come, yes?'

I looked over at my mother-in-law, thankful that she wasn't wielding her wooden spoon just now, although she was waving a spatula around somewhat menacingly.

'So, tell me about the job,' Sanjay said to me later, as we lay on our bed, watching television. 'Are you enjoying it so far? You know, if you don't we can find you something else.'

'No, no, I really like it. The people seem nice – at least the four that I've met so far. And it's *such* a great

50

place. They run all these different magazines, and even some TV thing, and I work on the floor of a magazine called *Hollywood Insider*, which reports on celebrities and movies.'

'Wow! Do you think you'll ever get to meet anyone famous?' Sanjay asked.

'I doubt it. I'm just a girl answering the phones in reception. But I really am enjoying it,' I said, snuggling up to him and enjoying the privacy of our bedroom. I knew it would be short-lived; in an hour, as was his habit every night, my father-in-law would summon me downstairs to make hot *pista* milk for him. And once I was in the kitchen, my mother-in-law always found something else for me to do.

'Hey, I have a great idea!' Sanjay exclaimed. 'I've always wanted to get one of those deals where we make bags for when a movie comes out – you know, with cartoon characters and stuff. Now that you know these people at the studios, maybe you can help me do that, introduce me to the right people. Shall I give you some samples to take into the office tomorrow?'

'Sanjay, I don't know if that's appropriate,' I said. 'And I don't know these people. I'm just a receptionist there. How can I carry a load of bags in tomorrow as if I'm selling something. It looks a bit tacky, no?'

Sanjay thought about it for a minute. 'Hah, maybe you're right,' he said. 'It's too soon. Let's wait a few months. I hope you'll still be there by then.'

'I hope so also,' I said. 'But you know, there is one

thing. I know it's my first day and all, but I think I'll be needing some new clothes. The people who work there are very fashionable. Not that I have to be very fancy-fancy or anything, but just something that looks a little more decent than what I have now. Do you think that would be OK?'

'I think so,' Sanjay said, wrapping his arm around me. 'We'll talk to Mummy and Papa about it and get their permission. You know how they feel about Western clothes. But maybe they'll agree. Then this weekend, if we have time, we'll go shopping.'

I was up at six the next morning, making the tea, which I stored in a Thermos, pending the awakening of the rest of the household, and left slices of bouncy white bread ready to be toasted in the miniature oven. Then I got going on dinner, which wasn't to be served for another fourteen hours, but at least prepared all the vegetables and left them covered in the refrigerator so my mother-in-law could cook them later. I unloaded the dishwasher from the night before, put everything away, cleaned the counters and was running upstairs to take a shower when Malini emerged from her room.

She was in a pair of white pyjamas with little red lips printed all over them, the top held up with two small straps, her nipples showing through underneath. I knew she was only wearing them because her parents were still asleep. As soon as they awoke, she would run into her room and throw on a dressing gown. Now, she yawned and stretched, revealing the tiny silver ring clipped through her belly button. I looked down at my high-collared floral nightgown and felt like an over-stuffed chintz sofa.

'Have a great day at work, *bhabi*,' she said. I had always thought that she looked, dressed and sounded like one of those girls on *Beverly Hills 90210*. I couldn't know for sure, but I wouldn't be surprised if, when nobody was looking, she acted like one of them too.

'Thank you, Malini,' I said, as I sprinted back into our bedroom. 'You have a nice day too.'

I found a place to park in the shade right beneath the building, and noted that it was exactly nine seventeen. I pulled out a Wet Wipe from the glove compartment, and ran it down my hair, removing the *sindoor* I had just applied before leaving the house. I had a small silver container of it in my bag, and would replace it later before I went home.

Office hours were nine thirty to five thirty, so I was early. I even had time to do what all the other early arrivals around me were doing – buying coffee and a pastry from a stall on wheels outside the entrance to the building.

Settling in behind my desk, I sat and waited for the phones to start ringing, for people to start coming through, for deliveries to pile up. At nine thirty on the dot, it seemed as if the whole place jolted awake and came to life. I could hear phones jingling all over the office, and the little system on my desk was flashing and beeping too. The doors swung open every minute or so, the reporters and researchers and photographers filing in, carrying computer bags and trendy totes and chatting with each other, occasionally and unthinkingly throwing a smile my way. I sat behind my desk and wanted to greet them all individually, making eye contact and nodding my head eagerly.

'Good morning,' I said, as they whisked by me, on their way to their offices. The only people who stopped to chat were Lou and Jerry, both asking me how I was settling in or if I needed anything.

'I'm doing fine, sir,' I said to Lou, who had already asked me four times not to call him that.

It wasn't too hard to feel invisible; all day long, people stood around me and chatted as if I wasn't there.

'So, did you get your period yet?' one girl in a short white skirt and black boots asked another. 'You must be *freaking* out! Does Simon know? Are you gonna tell him, or wait until you know for sure? I mean, you don't want him to marry you only because you might be pregnant, right?'

I cowered beneath the counter, answering phones, but couldn't help overhearing every word.

'He'll probably dump me,' the other girl replied. 'Don't think he's ready for any big commitment, you know? I'm screwed,' she said, turning paler than she already was and shaking her head. 'Anyway, forget all that. How are you and Patrick doing?'

'Yeah, great. He wants to go on holiday, asked me to pick where. There's a place I keep hearing about, but don't know too much about it. The West Bank?'

Later, in the elevator, I saw the same two women, still talking. When I got in with them, they stopped for a second, looked me up and down, and proceeded on their conversation, evidently deciding that I was too simple-minded to pay any heed. I stood in one corner, staring down at the light blue-with-black-trim salwar kameez, which was one of the nicest outfits from my trousseau. I thought I looked smart, and was hoping that the girls might comment on the exotica of my dress sense, but they said nothing, instead carrying on with their chat about missed menstruations and sun-tanning on the Gaza Strip.

Deanna was my only real link between the desk that I sat behind, and the far more vivid world that seemed to exist beyond it. During her four-a-day visits, she would tell me stories about people I hadn't spoken to, and give me glimmers of insight into the lives of colleagues that I would probably never meet.

'And that girl, Aimee, you know, the one who covers the nightclub scene, tall, skinny, blonde, beautiful, makes you sick just to look at her? You know? *Anyway*, she snuck her boyfriend in here, and was caught making out with him on the desk of the photo editor, who now wants to move out of his office because he says he can't imagine using that desk again! Can you believe it? Hysterical!' she said, as I stared at her, baffled at the things that went on in corporate America.

'*And*,' she continued, pausing for emphasis, 'that over-weight movie reviewer – you know the one, really serious, thinks he knows everything, total snob – he's about to get fired because they found out he was taking money from a studio to write good reviews. Isn't that *outrageous?*' she screamed, giggling.

'Not really,' I replied, whispering. 'In India, everyone does that.'

7

If everything were exactly according to the order of Hindu cultural law, I shouldn't really be living in America.

I shouldn't really even be married.

I am the youngest of four girls – which some would say is a disaster in itself. But, until a couple of months ago, I was also the youngest of four *unmarried* girls, which is something that parents with a weaker spiritual constitution than mine might forever be on Prozac for.

Where I come from, these things happen chronologically. Sisters get married in succession. The youngest waits her turn.

But by the time I was twenty-four, and my sisters still weren't married, my parents just didn't see how they could turn the offer down.

My mother never listened when she was told she had been cursed. Multiple girls, no sons, everyone kept saying, as if she needed reminding. But she simply shrugged, smiled, shook her head and patted ours. She called us her 'little Laxmis'.

'Just you see,' she said to all those who tut-tutted at her perceived misfortune. 'My girls will bring us great luck and joy. Just you see.'

She was right, and she was wrong. The luck came as my father's small construction business grew at a steady pace, and he was able to provide somewhat comfortably for us. But the joy faded as we grew older and our hands remained, mostly, unasked for, our hearts unattached, our dowries ready-in-waiting for years upon years.

We are all exactly two years apart in age, all of us born in the same last week of December, which made birthday parties convenient, if rather chaotic.

According to my grandmother, at the naming ceremonies for each, our family priest had cautioned my parents against giving any of us names that began with an R.

'It doesn't match your own initials,' he'd said, consulting his almanac. 'It will surely spell disaster on some level.' But my mother, who pooh-poohed anything to do with the occult, stood her ground. She adored the idea of having a gorgeous, voluptuous 'Rrrrr' trip off her tongue each time she might call her girls to her.

But by the time I came along, my mother relented and listened to the priest. 'P,' he said to her, calmly. 'Pooja, Payal, Pinky, anything like that will do.'

'Priyanka,' my mother announced. She had decided

to name me after the only daughter of Rajiv and Sonia Gandhi, the beloved assassinated prime minister and his white-skinned wife. But growing up, it was clear that nobody could see any resemblance between me and the charming, strong-willed scion of a legendary political family, so it didn't surprise me that, eventually, 'Priyanka' became simply 'Priya' – smaller, softer, far less regal-sounding.

I am convinced that the reason I am married today, and my sisters are not, is because of the name I was given at birth.

The letter had arrived at our home from a family friend in Bombay, telling us about a particular family in Los Angeles with a son about my age, who happened to have matrimony on his mind.

'I don't know, Chandru,' my mother had said to my father. 'Priya is our baby. She's our youngest.'

But my grandmother, whom everyone lovingly called Kaki (her given name was actually Kiku, but it required quite a deft use of the tongue to refer to her as Kaki Kiku) immediately demurred.

'Saras, our Priya is twenty-four already. She is hardly a baby. I hear this family that is asking for her, they are quite good people. They have their own business. I think you should definitely consider it.'

Later that day, I heard my grandmother on the phone with the go-between in Bombay, as if she needed to convince him further of my virtues. I watched her small, grey-haired head bobbing in enthusiasm, her slim spectacles sliding down a perfect and pointed nose.

As far as Kaki saw it, I had inherited a little bit of everyone's best. Radha was born beautiful, Roma was blessed with what is often described as 'a good nature', and Ria had copious quantities of spirit. Kaki always told me that these characteristics seemed to have been distilled and diluted and poured into me.

'Oh, and our Priya is *quite* pretty,' I heard her say, 'and really rather positive in terms of outlook, always smiling and that. And a straightforward sort of girl, no nonsense and hanky-panky. Quiet, but outspoken if she has to be, which is rarely. Touch wood, touch wood, she is a *lovely* girl.' Kaki reached over and laid her hand on the teak coffee table. She did so frequently, at every opportune and necessary moment, like when letting people know that my father had secured another construction project – 'God has been good to him, touch wood.' She knew, and had taught us all, that trumpeting our accomplishments and singing our own praises without then fingering something derived from a tree to ward off the evil eye would no doubt result in calamity and downfall.

'Everybody knows, darling,' she used to say to me, 'that for good fortune to remain, humility must always be present. No matter what wonder life brings you, do not ever be boastful.'

Now, as Kaki made her grandmotherly efforts to sell

me over the phone, my mother and I took a jug of lime water and went out into the small garden behind our house, where yesterday's washing still flapped in the breeze. My mother ran her hand through her long, full hair and turned to look at me as I swung lazily in the old rusty swing.

My mother was, in many ways, quite modern. She resisted the stereotype of Indian motherhood, shunning saris in favour of trousers and long tops when she was at home, and *lassis* for gin and tonic when no one was looking. But when it came to us girls, she tacitly agreed with my father about the most appropriate way to bring us up, the concealing clothes we should wear and the restrictions we were to put on our own minds. She nodded when my father said that the only way for us girls to remain 'unspoiled' was to be sheltered from anything that lay beyond our house in Delhi's Defence Colony, where we knew all the neighbours' names. The city had its society girls, the ones with the halter-tops, who went disco dancing. They lived on the leafy streets of Nizamuddin East and inside the grand houses of Jangpura Extension, with their sprawling lawns. They sat in imported cars, windows slightly lowered, atop which pecked cigarettes suspended between manicured fingers. They were Indian girls like us, yet as foreign as anything.

Despite all the protection and purity, however – or perhaps as a result of it – we had remained single. My parents had been keen to keep us close by, so initially

61

had sought out boys only from Delhi. They had envisioned a life for us where we would be able to stop by at our natal home, our babies in our arms, and have clattering Sunday family lunches, a mélange of sons-in-law and grandchildren. But then Kaki insisted that the radius be extended to the rest of India, and then, a couple of years later, pulled out even further to other parts of Asia – Bangkok or Hong Kong maybe, some place just a few hours by plane away, with little jet lag involved.

But when the letter came from my father's friend in Bombay, speaking of a boy in *America*, of all places, my father's first instinct was to ignore it, before Kaki changed his mind.

'Houses are big there,' she said. 'And everything is available. And no blackouts and rations like we still have here. It is far, but it could be a good life for our Priya. At least let the boy and girl exchange photos.'

When his arrived, I thought Sanjay looked like the kind of boy who might still be living on our street, the boy-next-door type I might have fallen in love with. He had a sweet smile, beautiful features, hair that fell into his eyes with an endearing innocence. I remember nodding in agreement, which is why he called me one day, at a prearranged time. I blushed as I heard his voice echoing down the static-filled telephone line, my sisters and parents gathered all around me. Sanjay told me a little of his life in California, and it seemed respectable and appealing. He had been there since he was five, so was more American than Indian.

Afterwards, I wasn't sure what to think or how to respond. I was a twenty-four-year-old jobless virgin, who had hardly been trained to make decisions and have ideas and know truth from fantasy. But everyone around me was so excited – sisters talking about buying new saris, mother planning on sending out baskets of sweets in celebration, grandmother doing prayers of gratitude in the temple – that I got swept along with it. Without ever really planning it, I found myself engaged.

Sanjay and I met for the first time a week before our wedding, at the engagement ceremony. He came straight from the airport, a baseball cap on his head and bright red socks on his feet. He looked happy and excited, as if this was going to be like a day at Disneyland. He reached out his hand for mine and shook it, eagerly looking at my face.

'You are very pretty,' he said, looking relieved. 'Even prettier than your photo.' I smiled, taking in his handsome features and easy smile. We exchanged garlands in front of a large marble statue of Lord Shiva and his consort, Parvati, and I thought that, like the heavenly beings, we made quite a match. We may have only just met, but I was quite sure that I would love him in no time.

The six days between our meeting and the wedding were mostly happy. We shyly avoided kisses, but occasionally allowed our fingers to touch as we stood behind the pillars in my home, while my relatives golden-fried sugary *jalebis* and florists fussed around the rooms. The neighbourhood children would show up at our door for the chocolates and foil-wrapped hard-boiled sweets that were generously distributed at wedding times. They would gather around and gleefully sing the childish tunes that they always brought out for these occasions: 'Sanjay and Priya sitting in a tree, K-I-S-S-I-N-G, first comes love, then comes marriage, then comes baby in a golden carriage!' before scampering off, their pockets bulging with sweets. Their mischievous exhortations aside, Sanjay and I observed cultural norms and restrained ourselves from overt shows of affection. Even so, everyone told us we looked as happy as two toddlers playing in a park on a summer's afternoon.

My delight notwithstanding, the presence of Sanjay's mother always weighed me down. I appeared to have been the last one to find out about her bitter nature. 'Oh, she's marrying *Nita's* son, is she?' people would ask my parents, trying to hide the astonishment in their eyes. 'The boy is very handsome, yes, yes. And the family is *quite* well off, we believe. But that mother . . .' I overheard one of my many interfering, melodramatic aunts warning my father that eventually Nita's miserable temperament would manifest in her children.

'The milk that flowed through her breasts must surely have been sour, smelling like lime,' said the aunt. 'How do we know that Sanjay did not receive this bad milk, which must have fizzled in his stomach like bad curd?

How do we know he will not grow up to be like his mother? Our Priya will have to work extra hard to keep him sweet.'

To me, my mother-in-law was often mean and critical, condemning me a few days before our wedding because my outfit was 'too revealing' and my collarbone was showing.

'My parents are very conservative,' Sanjay had said to me. 'They want you to dress only in Indian clothes. You understand, no?'

Two days prior to wedding, when we were out being showered with good wishes by friends, dining and dancing and drinking (Sanjay had beer, I stuck to Shirley Temples), Sanjay announced that he had to get home early because he had promised his mother. And that whole week long, she would call and demand extra additions to the dowry, the supplying of which had taxed my parents enough.

I should have taken that as my cue to end things.

But I couldn't.

My family had already been through enough with so many unmarried daughters, and I was not about to bring more shame on their heads.

Plus, the neighbourhood children were right. I felt as if I loved Sanjay. And following love must come marriage.

And as my Aunt Vimla would insist: 'All Indian families are the same. Mothers want the best for their sons. Be obedient and homely, and everything will be fine. Things always get better after marriage.'

At the wedding, I was surprised that they didn't make me change my name. Hindu brides don't simply take on their husband's surname, but a new first and middle appellation as well. I was to go from Priyanka Chandru Mehta to something else entirely. My original middle name was my father's name, now to be replaced by my husband's name, for as Kaki had explained to me, this was a significant indicator that Hindu girls are 'to go from their father's house to their husband's house, and nowhere in between'. And the point of changing my first name was simply to show that my identity – or what little of it I had – would be shed alongside my virginity. With a slim gold band on my finger, and the black-beaded *mangal sutra* necklace that all Hindu brides are given, I was to become a brand-new person. As Sanjay and I sat in front of the fire, its grey smoke twirling overhead, I waited for the priest to whisper my new name into my ear. But he did not. As it turned out, Priya was the perfect fit, as far as names go, for Sanjay. I would be Priya Sanjay Sohni. One out of three wasn't bad.

Right after the wedding, the *dholi* was waiting for me outside the temple where the nuptials had taken place. I used to dream about being carried off in this palanquin, excitedly anticipating my life ahead with a new husband; only, I had always thought that I would have watched all my sisters make the journey before me. Instead, now, they each hugged me in turn, their cheeks wet with tears against my own. Aunt Vimla, who was a distant cousin to my mother but seemed to have turned herself into the family know-it-all, elbowed her way towards me and whispered in my ear: 'Something will happen to you when you are alone together. Don't cry, even if there is pain. We have all done it. And remember, you have married not just Sanjay but his entire family. You must do everything to please them. Only then will you have blessings on your head.'

My mother, however, had pushed Vimla aside, and clasped her strong arms around my neck. 'My darling daughter, you are my first child to be married, but, please God, may you not be the last. May you stay happy. And if ever you are not, remember you always have a home with us.' But then my mother paused, cupped the back of my head with her hand, stared straight into my eyes, and said: 'But, Priya, darling, *do* try and be happy.'

Inside the *dholi*, I hugged my knees towards me, and fingered the coarse, wiry golden threads of my sari. I pulled aside the strings of jasmine that quivered in the warm evening breeze, and waited quietly as everyone paid their respects to a young, departing bride. Vimla and her entourage were meant to cry at the sight of me leaving, but instead they were rejoicing. They were waving and cheering, as if suddenly relieved of some monumental burden. I could swear that I even heard one of them yell out: 'See ya!'

Minutes later, I arrived at the home that Sanjay and his family had rented for the wedding. As they heard me approach, his parents and other family members stepped out of their ground-floor apartment, ready to welcome me in for the next ceremony. My mother-in-law placed a copper urn filled with water in my palms. I immersed one hand into the clear cool liquid, and flicked droplets around the room as I stepped over the threshold. New brides, so it is believed, have the power to bless homes and households, and so are treated like goddesses. That, for the most part, is something that quickly wears off.

My in-laws coaxed me into a chair for the *datar* ceremony, during which handfuls of salt are exchanged with each and every member of the family I had just married into, in a ritual symbolizing give and take.

As I rubbed off the rough grains from my reddened palms, I suspected then that that too would soon become another untruth.

In the end, it was a pair of shoes and a plastic statue of doves that convinced me that I should be married.

Years ago, my father had been given a pair of Bally shoes by a rich relative who had returned from a holiday in Switzerland. 'I will wear these to the marriage of my first daughter,' he had said proudly, holding up the shiny onyx-black polished leather shoes as if they were an award.

But for five years, the shoes lay in their box, itself covered in a fine layer of powdery dust. At each formal occasion that arrived in Delhi, my mother would encourage him to take them out and wear them.

'I will wait,' he said quietly. 'These were gifted to me for a reason, and I will wait for the reason to happen.'

Down the street in my grandparents' home, Kaki had – on the centre of her dining table – a figurine of four doves, two crouching, two poised for flight.

'These birds are like all of you,' she would say to us. 'Some are babies still –' and she would stroke Ria's head and mine – 'and others are ready to leave the nest,' she wailed, looking over at Radha and Roma. 'When, oh when, will my birds fly to homes of their own?' she would cry dramatically, sobbing into the folds of her sari.

At my wedding, my father strutted around in his shiny black shoes, seemingly more proud of what he wore on his feet than of the family he had chosen for me to marry into. And thereafter, Kaki rubbed and petted the smallest of the doves, thinking that maybe doing so would ensure that I would never return.

8

Less than a week into my job, it became apparent to me that Lynette Dove ran this place. She was in charge of movie coverage – what interviews ran, how much space they got, which pictures were used – and so she received the most elaborate baskets of edibles from studios, and lush, fragrant floral arrangements from publicists, all of which sat on the counter above my desk pending her showing up to claim them. Judging by the amount of mail she got, she was invited to everything that happened in this town, and was so important to the magazine that it seemed to revolve entirely around her.

I had seen Lynette Dove my third day at work, when she breezed into the office followed by her assistant, a gorgeous young black woman who looked like she was a missing member of Destiny's Child. Deanna had been standing by my desk chatting, as always, and the appearance of the woman the junior staff here called Ms Dove prompted Deanna to tell me about what she called 'the Legend of Lynette'.

'She's been here since the day this magazine started,' Deanna said, whispering. 'There's just something about her. She's so clever and smart and sophisticated. Everyone wants to meet her. I've been working here two years, and I've never even gotten close to the woman,' she said.

Lynette *looked* like the sort of person who would be a good writer. There was something trim and efficient about her, as if nothing in her home, office or life would ever be out of place, that she would always be able to find her keys and that fresh bottles of water would be ready for her in her car, and that she would never cry at night, no matter how lonely she was, no matter who she was without.

She wore her shiny dark brown hair straight to just below her shoulders, all sleek and tidy. She was dressed in tailored slacks made from beautiful silk fabric, cut close to the leg, set off with high heels. Her top was casual, featuring an image of Buddha, topped off with an expensive-looking jacket.

I looked at her with admiration – that here was a woman who knew not only how to write, but also, evidently, how to dress.

She whizzed by my desk straight into her office, but her assistant stopped to see if there were any messages.

I handed over a few that had come through to the main switchboard because Lynette's voicemail was full, and also gave the assistant two bouquets of flowers that had arrived that morning.

'Thanks,' she said, smiling widely. 'I'd better run after her. Talk to you later.'

True to her word, the assistant did stop by my desk at lunchtime, when things were quieter.

'Didn't get a chance to say hi,' she said. 'So hi!' and she beamed a big, broad smile. 'My name is Shanisse. You're new here, right? I always make it a point to get to know every single receptionist who works here, even if they're gone after a couple of months. Hope you stick around!' she said.

'Oh yes, indeed, I plan to,' I said, standing up. 'Hello, my name is Priya. Very nice to meet you.'

'Thanks for looking after all that stuff earlier. I know sometimes it piles up. Lynette often works from home and doesn't always come in, so there's a bit of a backlog with her messages and flowers and stuff.'

'That's OK,' I said. 'It's my job. She seems very busy.'

'She is. I don't expect you to know this, but she kinda runs things here. Nothing happens without Lynette knowing about it.

'Look, it's after one and I haven't had time to eat,' she continued. 'Wanna run out and grab a sandwich?'

I had actually brought lunch in with me – I couldn't afford to eat out everyday, like most of the people here did. But someone, for once, was asking me to go out with them, and I feared that if I said no, nobody would ever ask me again.

We looked quite a pair walking down the street, she in her fitted trousers that clung to her bottom, a scooped-neck top that revealed just a hint of a black lace bra, and high heels, and me in a mustard-coloured salwar kameez with tiny red polka dots and the fake Dr Scholls that I had found in a Delhi market. I realized then that Shanisse was the first black person I had ever had a full conversation with; there is not a large African-American community in India.

'I like what you're wearing,' Shanisse said, as we neared the restaurant, the Italian café I had eaten in on my first day here. 'It's funky, and comfortable-looking. I gotta be careful – my pants are so tight that if I so much as sneeze, they're liable to tear right off me and fly across the room.'

I stuck to a small salad while Shanisse ordered a focaccia and asked the server to make it quick.

'I'm starved,' she said. 'Lynette has me running around like a maniac. I barely get time to go to the ladies' room,' she laughed.

'So, where are you from? As soon as I heard you speak, I thought you had such a great accent. British, is it?'

'Somewhat,' I replied. 'I'm from India, but went to a convent school in Delhi so came out with this odd Anglo-Indian accent.'

'I've never been to India. Would love to go. How long you been in this country?'

I told Shanisse my story – about my whirlwind arranged marriage to a man I met a week before our

74

wedding, and she swallowed her food noisily and dropped her mouth open. I even brought out the photograph of Sanjay and me on our wedding day that I kept in my wallet, and her eyes opened wide with delight.

'Love the clothes,' she said, looking at my burgundy-and-gold sari, and Sanjay's high-collared cream brocade jacket. 'Wow, does he have dimples! He sure is cute! I'd marry him in a second as well! Although, gotta tell you, don't know about the living arrangements. For me, that'd be newlywed suicide. The marriage wouldn't have a hope in hell of lasting five minutes.'

'It's not so bad,' I said. 'It's a little inconvenient sometimes, and my in-laws can be demanding, and there are days when I wished Sanjay and I had more privacy. We can't even fight in peace,' I said, smiling. 'But at least there is a support system. We look after one another.'

'Well, if you want to get out of the house more, then maybe after a year you can apply for an intern position at the *Insider*,' she said, 'and then work up to editorial assistant. Most receptionists go off and try and get into acting, but the others apply to be interns. It's a great way to get your foot in.'

'No, that wouldn't happen in my case,' I said, finishing the last of my salad. 'I have always longed to be a journalist, but my in-laws are pretty strict. They don't mind me being a receptionist, but that's it. They don't think it's appropriate for a newlywed woman to be going here and there alone, meeting with strange people. They forbid it. Maybe in my next life.'

'You know, I gotta tell you, I think they have a point,' said Shanisse. 'My boyfriend, Michael, and I fight constantly about my long hours, the unpredictability of the job. It's really demanding work. At least you can keep reasonable hours now. But Lynette and I don't know where we're going to be one day to the next. You can't really live like that if you have a family counting on you.'

Shanisse wasn't technically just Lynette Dove's assistant; her official title was 'Entertainment Correspondent – Movies' – a 'junior' to Lynette's 'senior'. She didn't only deliver her boss's messages and put newly arrived flowers in vases but she went out and did stories, interviewed Hollywood people, attended screenings and premieres. She did confess that she got Lynette's 'castoffs' – the things that her boss was too busy or preoccupied to fit in or just not interested in doing.

'There is just so much that goes on in this town that Lynette can't be at everything,' she said. 'There are set visits, junkets, opening nights and charity events that are tied to films. It goes on and on. You'll see. You'll learn how things work in no time.'

Shanisse asked for the bill and insisted on paying all of it, saying that she was going to 'expense' it.

'Lynette has told me to get to know all the new girls, the receptionists and editorial assistants,' she said. 'Makes life easier in our department when we know we're all on the same page.'

***

The weekend rolled around quicker than it usually did when I was a stay-at-home wife, when it didn't really matter what day of the week it was, as it was always the same. Now, before I knew it, it was Friday evening, and although it was a colossal effort making it home before dinner-time because obviously everybody in Los Angeles was trying to do the same, I was pleased to have the weekend off. Well, 'off' wasn't really an accurate term, given that there was so much housework to catch up on. Shanisse, a single working woman, had a cleaning lady come in once a week to tidy up her one-bedroomed condo. But my mother-in-law had always been adamantly against having what she called 'outside help', even if I was now holding down a full-time job.

'Those people steal things,' she had said to me. 'And they don't do anything right. If we want to look after our house a particular way, we have to do it ourselves,' she'd added, as Malini slinked off into her bedroom with yet another magazine. My sister-in-law had just completed a course in artistic make-up application – she had said it was her dream to make the movie stars even more beautiful. But my father-in-law had thought this to be unseemly work for a girl of good standing, and had suggested she take some time off before deciding what to do next, evidently hoping that marriage would happen to her as easily as it had happened to me. So, for now, Malini spent lots of her time in beauty salons and nail bars, doing what she called 'professional research'. But at least, as a result of it, she always looked good.

After I had finished all the household chores the next morning, I woke Sanjay up.

'Honey, what time is it?' he asked sleepily.

'It's after eleven already. Come on, get up. Maybe we can go out for lunch and then go buy some new clothes. I've already been working almost a week, and I feel really odd being the only girl there in Indian clothes. Did you talk to your parents about me buying a few Western things?'

'Not yet,' he said, throwing off the covers. 'We'll ask them now.'

By the time we gathered ourselves, showered, dressed, did a brief morning prayer in the small temple fitted into a corner of the hallway and went downstairs, it was close to noon. My in-laws and Malini were already up and about, trying to decide what to have me make for lunch.

'Where are you going?' my mother-in-law asked.

'We thought we'd go and do some shopping. Priya needs a few new clothes for work,' he informed them.

'What kind of clothes?' my father-in-law asked, putting down his newspaper. 'You are the daughter-in-law of this house, and you must dress correctly. We can't have people talking.'

'Of course, Papa,' I said. 'But I thought maybe I could

find something Western, but still covered, not at all revealing or anything.'

'Nothing wrong with Indian clothes,' my father-in-law insisted. 'But if you want to go look around, fine. We'll also come. First we'll go out for lunch, then clothes.'

Ten minutes later, all five of us were piled into Sanjay's car. I was craving Chinese food, but they preferred Indian, so, being outnumbered four to one, we ended up with *paneer* and *pakora*.

I had wanted to go to the mall, one I had wandered through a few weeks ago after grocery shopping, and where I knew Malini bought all the spiffy, sexy little clothes that she kept hidden under long coats, even in the height of summer. At those boutiques, I had seen dark red leather skirts that curved against the body, clingy little tops, and jeans that hung so low on the girls who were trying them on that I was almost too ashamed to look.

But my mother-in-law had another idea. So while we were still digesting deep-fried Indian food, we pulled up in front of Ross, a warehouse-like store where discounted duds spill from racks.

'You can find great buys here if you have the patience to look,' said Malini. 'Don't worry, *bhabi*, no more Bhopal village girl look for you.' She stayed close to my side as my father-in-law went straight to the women's clothes section, and pulled out a pair of blue trousers with an elastic waistband.

'How's this, Priya?' he said, holding them up.

'Professional, simple. I think you'll look very nice in them.'

'Please, Papa, that's pretty sad,' Malini replied, on my behalf. 'They've got all the flair of a garden hose. We need something with a bit more colour.'

My mother-in-law had been stationed by the dress section, and held up an ankle-length pinafore-frock covered in orange and yellow flowers.

'Oh, that's quite pretty,' I said to Malini, who grabbed it out of her mother's hands and exclaimed: 'This is so hideous that not even a colour-blind, overweight, pregnant-with-triplets woman would wear it.

'Look, *bhabi*, come with me,' she said, telling her parents to go and browse through the home furnishings department.

Together with Sanjay, we strolled down the aisles, pushing through hundreds of jackets and skirts and tops and blazers and jeans. Malini filled a blue shopping cart with possibilities and then held them up in front of her parents. I recognized them for the kinds of things I had seen in her own wardrobe. But now, they were all individually rejected for being 'too showy', 'too low-cut', 'too short', 'too tight', 'too fancy.'

'Mum, Papa, you're being ridiculous,' she said. 'These are just fun things. What's the problem?'

'Priya is the daughter-in-law,' her father replied sternly. 'What you are showing us is for low-class American girls.'

I guessed, at that point, that my mother-in-law hadn't looked inside Malini's wardrobe lately.

We gave up and went home, and I resigned myself to another week of looking like a reject in a Miss Tamil Nadu contest.

9

Sunday was usually speak-to-family day. My sisters called from Delhi at around the same time every Sunday evening, and I would take the call in our bedroom so I wouldn't have my in-laws listening to every word, which they did while pretending to be watching *The Simpsons*. Talking to my family was the highlight of my week, with all of us drowning in delight at the minutia of one another's lives: my mother thrilled to hear me talk about the recipe for *sag paneer* I had just tried out, my father curious to know how Sanjay's bag business was doing, my sisters wanting to know everything about my new life, while I enquired about the servants I had grown up with, what had become of the books I was forced to leave behind, and if the twine rope I used to swing from on my favourite tree in our garden was just as I had left it.

'The women here are not afraid to drive big cars, like trucks,' I had told my sister Roma my first weekend in

America. 'They drink beer. And then, like I was reading in some magazines, sometimes they get married . . . to *each other*!'

When I had first started looking for a job and told my father, he had grunted down the phone line, miffed until I gently explained to him that this was America, and everyone here worked.

'What kind of a family have I married you into?' he first asked. 'Forcing a good girl like you to take a job?'

'Oh, Daddy, please, I really don't mind it,' I said to him. 'I will find something decent and respectable. Working is part of life here.'

The day that I started my job I had called them, so excited that the words just tumbled out of my mouth, leaving my mother staggered and still rather confused about what I actually did.

'Darling, all I heard was something about Harrison Ford and answering phones. Are you working for him, sweetheart?'

Of my three sisters, I was closest to Radha, the eldest. Every week when we spoke, she asked me about married life, what Sanjay and I had done that weekend, what revelations I had come to about love, and unity, and commitment. She was, in many ways, living through me. And it saddened me that it wasn't the other way around – that I, as the youngest sister, wasn't seeking the insights of the eldest.

'What's it like?' Radha asked me again. 'That country, your house, your life. Tell me.' Since getting married, I

84

had suddenly felt like the first-born, endowed with a maturity and sophistication that I didn't deserve. 'And marriage? What is marriage like?'

'I suppose the best thing about it is that I don't have to think about what to do on New Year's Eve,' I said, remembering how us girls would stare out the window as young dressed-up couples from our street got into their cars and went off for a night of partying to mark the end of another year. Silently, we all longed to be among them.

'I think there is more to it than that,' Radha said quietly. 'You may not see it now, but you are a very lucky girl to have someone you can at least try to love.'

To this day, people still tut-tutted and tsk-tsked when they talked about Radha. Just this evening, after she had called, my mother-in-law had asked me 'how Radha is feeling'.

As if what happened to her had happened yesterday. To my sister, I know it still felt that way.

When it happened, Radha was twenty, and stunning. She was as willowy as one of the canes that grew in the sugar fields, and as sweet. She sprang out of bed in the mornings smelling like jasmine and tiptoed through the house with steps as soft as whispers. Her smile filled the sun-room at high noon, bringing light to a face that was already as creamy white as the sheets she slept on. It was no surprise that to my mother, she was 'Radiant Radha'.

She had been named after the lifelong love and consort

of Lord Krishna, one of Hinduism's most favoured deities. So it was fitting that she found a veritable god of a fiancé. His name was Nishant, and he was descended from a dynasty of warrior princes who had, in the twentieth century, made a fortune in land, logging and ice-cream parlours across the country. He and his younger brother, Nayan, were the best and brightest bachelors around.

Radha and Nishant met at a dinner party, soon after she had turned nineteen. He was four years older, four inches taller, and as strong and noble and kind as anyone would have picked out for her. When the two of them were introduced, everyone in the room turned to look at them. My mother gasped when she saw her eldest child come face-to-face with the young modern-day prince. It was as if, she said later, Radha had found the other half of her soul in Nishant.

Their engagement was announced three weeks later, and Delhi lit up at the news. It was going to be the conjoining of two beauties, two pure hearts, a lovely and humble girl being sought after by a solid and wealthy family who wanted no dowry, just her.

My sisters and I called Nishant *jijaji* – 'big brother' – and we loved him like one. Nayan became like a close cousin, although Kaki was a great believer in sisters marrying into the same family, and had delicately dropped hints to Nishant's parents that perhaps Roma might be a good match for brother number two, eventually.

The night before the wedding, the celebrations at Nishant's home were at their height. Three hundred people danced on the green lawns, which had been covered by gold-tasselled tents strung atop beribboned maypoles. My mother had stood on a velvet-sheathed podium and sung a song to her beloved eldest daughter, a song of farewell and longing and profound hope. Radha had cried, and then laughed again when Nishant put his arm around her and kissed her on her forehead. Everyone danced in a whirl of magenta saris and beaded brocades and harmonium chords, trumpets blaring and fireworks filling the star-stroked sky.

Radha was drunk on joy, and Nishant on champagne.

At two in the morning, Nishant brought Radha home. She retired to her room, determined to get some sleep before the wedding the next day. As I said good night to her, she kissed a framed photograph of Nishant that stood on her bedside table, and pressed it close to her chest, snuggled down under her sheets with it, and went to sleep.

An hour later, precisely 3.11 a.m., the phone rang, sharp and sudden through the still and darkened house, endless, like village church bells on Christmas morning. I was fourteen years old, scared, standing at the top of the staircase, watching as my father answered, listened silently for a moment, and then dropped the receiver so it banged against the cold floor. He hung his head, cried into his *kurta* and climbed back up the stairs as frail and pale as a man on his deathbed. He walked into his bedroom and spoke to my mother, and she screamed. They both came out, ashen as the early morning sky, and went into Radha's room. I heard deep, piercing cries, the sound of glass shattering, screeching threats of suicide. A doctor arrived, the servants hushed in and out, while my other sisters and I stood outside on the landing, too shocked to speak.

His car had hit a tree. It was instantaneous, we were told, as if that would make us feel better. He didn't suffer.

Radha wore white for a month after that. It is the colour of grief and widowhood, and while she and Nishant had yet to garland one another and be blessed by a priest, they felt that they were already married.

After that, her footsteps became sullen and heavy, her face pallid, her smile weak and small.

After that, she said she would never marry.

10

The red suitcase, its clasps long-rusted, had apparently remained in the attic untouched for years.

As soon as I got off the phone with my sisters and my mother, the bag was lying in the centre of our bedroom, covered in dust and smelling of mothballs.

'What is that suitcase for, Mummy?' I asked her, descending to the kitchen.

'I too was new here once,' she said. 'I had been married five years when we came to this country, but I was not much older than you. I, too, had to go through everything you are now going through.'

She looked at my puzzled face, and told me to go back upstairs.

'Just open it,' she said, looking proud. 'I think you will be happy with what you find inside.'

* * *

Polyester was big twenty years ago, and I was certain that the world's supply of it was sitting inside the dirty red suitcase.

My mother-in-law told me that, two decades ago, she had finally given in to the curious looks of strangers, and bought a Western wardrobe.

'It was not easy, being young in America and only in saris all day,' she said. 'I had supermarketing to do, banking to do. How to go everywhere and do everything, with people staring – staring?' she explained, as she lifted up each individual item, peeling it away from the one below it. 'I was thin then, like you.'

Sanjay sat on the edge of our bed, looking moved by his mother's generosity. I too was touched by the spirit in which she was offering me her old clothes. It was, if nothing else, a way for her to show that she commiserated.

'See? Very nice lace blouse,' she said, holding up a frilly confection that looked like the top part of a wedding dress, its shoulders puffy and sleeves slender. 'And see, these shiny belts were very popular, and now they are coming back in fashion,' she continued, displaying a black patent waist-cincher with a sparkling butterfly on the front.

'You can have all these,' she said, hugging me. 'You are like my daughter also, nah? You can also wear nice Western clothes. *Chalo*, when you go to the office tomorrow, you will look like a new girl, smart and fancy-fancy and all.'

* * *

90

It took most of the morning for it to register that, this time, the people around me *were* really laughing at me.

I had been so proud that day, stepping out of my car and into the marble foyer. I was dressed not just in Western clothes, but in what they fashionably call 'vintage' in these parts, according to Malini.

'It's *very* cool,' Malini had said to me. '*Lucky* magazine just did a big spread on it. Everything old is new again. You know, this stuff sells for a fortune in those stores on Melrose.'

I had no idea what she was talking about, but if Malini said that vintage was in, and that my mother-in-law's old clothes qualified as that, then who was I to argue with her?

But I should have taken her snigger, as I left the house, as the first sign. Instead of her customary, 'Have a great day, *bhabi*,' she ran to hide in the kitchen, giggling into her handkerchief as I walked by her, thinking at that moment that perhaps she was trying to stifle a sneeze.

And it wasn't until I was at my desk, a few hours later, that I fully understood what all the hilarity was about.

'Wow, you look, er, interesting,' Deanna said as she came by with her first deliveries of the day. 'Another fancy dress costume? Like those sarongs and things you wear?'

'Saris,' I said quietly, ashamed. 'Those are not fancy dress, and neither is this.'

In the ladies' room later, I ran into Shanisse, who cupped her hands around her mouth so I wouldn't see her jaw drop.

91

'Sorry,' she said to me, realizing I had noticed the look of horror on her face.

'What?' I asked her, now upset. 'Everyone seems to be laughing at me today. What?'

'Well, it's just your, um, outfit,' Shanisse said, stifling a laugh. 'It's, er, kinda unusual, I guess.'

I looked into the full-length mirror against one wall and didn't see what the joke was. From my mother-in-law's stash, I had chosen a long jersey skirt in bright red with a handkerchief hem, which I had thought was very pretty. With that, I wore a cream high-necked blouse that had little sparkly stones scattered all over the front, and a thick red belt that sat across my hips, decorated with a shiny gold heart. On my feet were the beige leather sandals I always wore, although my mother-in-law had suggested I wear heels to give my outfit what she described as 'some more extra style'. She even lent me her spongy foam curlers the night before, which I laced through my hair before going to bed, so this morning I had a slightly frizzy hairdo that was exactly like the one Drew Barrymore had on the cover of last week's magazine. To make mine extra special, my mother-in-law loaned me a red velvet bow, which I affixed to the top of my scalp.

All in all, I thought I looked rather nice.

'What's wrong?' I asked, looking alternately at the mirror and then up and down my outfit. 'Do you think maybe the shoes don't match? Or maybe the stockings look a bit funny through the open toes?'

'Honey, that's the least of your problems,' she said. 'Listen, don't take this the wrong way, but you look like a gypsy on speed. All that red and glitz and way too much bad dazzle for this time of day. Sweetie, all you need is a long-haired wig and you've got Cher. Know what I'm saying?'

I shook my head, confused and tearful.

'I just wanted to fit in,' I said.

'Girl, don't make plans for lunch today,' Shanisse replied, suddenly looking sorry for me. 'We're going shopping.'

On the way to the nearest mall, which was only a ten-minute drive from the office, I told her about my in-laws' refusal to let me dress like 'a normal American person', as I described it.

'Let's just get you some clothes first,' Shanisse said. 'And then we'll figure out a way for you to wear them without giving each member of your family a heart attack.'

I had never seen anyone pick out clothes so fast. While I stood on the sidelines, Shanisse threw hangers into a basket, looking at size tags, comparing prices, holding things up to me. She waited outside the fitting room as I tried everything on — the jeans similar to the ones she had, tailored trousers like I had seen on Lynette, a smart jacket made from fake suede, tops with pretty designs in ice-cream colours. I stepped outside for her approval, which she gave via an immediate nod or shake of the head. No hesitation, no considering. As I stood at the cash register, she went off and came back with little containers of blush and eyeshadows, two pairs of shoes and a small shoulder bag, plopped them down on the counter in front of me, and said: 'My treat.' Then she yanked me out of there to the Supercuts next door, and I cringed while they snipped two inches off my long hair, and Shanisse instructed them to 'give me layers'. As soon as we were back in the car, I put my big red velvet bow back on, as my friend rolled her eyes.

That night, before going home, I made a rare stop at the gym. I paid for a monthly locker, and rammed in two bags of clothes. As Shanisse had convinced me, there was no reason for my in-laws to see them – not yet anyway.

'Just get yourself organized so you can make it down to the gym in the morning to change, and do the same on the way back,' she counselled. 'And I'm sure they won't mind about the haircut. I mean, it's not like you look like a hussy or anything,' she said. 'Otherwise, the less they know, the better.'

11

It's true when they say that people who look good, feel good. The last time I had felt this pretty was on my wedding day.

When I got to work that day, and stepped onto the marble floor inside the double glass doors of the office, I felt as attractive as Malini, or even Brooke Shields. I had chosen a taupe skirt and a dusky pink top with beige print, cream-coloured sandals, and had tiny gold hoops in my ears that were from my trousseau but which I had never worn. The same shade of pink was on my lips and cheeks as I wore on my body, and my freshly washed, newly cut hair bounced in all the right places.

I had actually left for work this morning dressed in a loose thigh-length blue top and oversized white trousers, courtesy of the red suitcase, my hair tied up in a scrunchy. As I was running out of the house, my mother-in-law had told me that I 'looked nice', which was a generous observation.

Lou came through the doors just as I was sorting through the mail delivery.

'Good morning, Priya,' he said, carrying on to his office. He stopped for a second, looked at me again, and said: 'You look well rested.'

'Well rested.' My first compliment of the day.

Then Deanna strolled by, and was, as always, a hundred times more effusive.

'Priya! You look sensational! What did you do?' she screeched, asking me to stand up and twirl around. 'Love the outfit, love the look. You fit right in behind that smart-looking desk.'

'Sensational.' Compliment number two.

Dozens of other employees passed by, and perhaps I was imagining it, but it seemed that they noticed me more today than they had done in the past week. They smiled and nodded and threw casual 'hi's' my way before moving on, some of them stopping to pick up their messages.

At eleven, Lynette came tearing through the doors, her mobile affixed to her ear, scribbling something down on the back of a folder.

'Right, the two Toms, Brad, Denzel, Mel . . . great, who else is going to be there?' she clipped into the phone, scribbling as she went. She didn't look in my direction, heading straight towards her corner office. Five minutes later, Shanisse trailed behind.

'Would you believe she asked me to go park her car? She's *never* done that before. She must be really stressed out,' she said, looking a little miffed none the less. I mean, I have a degree from Columbia and now I'm a valet?' she repeated, clearly upset. 'Well, I'll let it go just this once, but I tell you . . . Wow, Priya, you look wonderful!' she exclaimed. 'What a huge difference! We did good, girl! *Now* you look like you belong here!'

'Belong here.' Compliment number three. And the best one so far.

At the end of my first three months at the *Hollywood Insider*, Hilda and Lou wanted to celebrate. Apart from Dara, no other receptionist had ever lasted that long.

'We hope you stick around for ever,' Lou said. 'We're thrilled with how you're working out.' I beamed in delight, and continued with my filing duties, as Lou left a box of chocolates on my desk.

My repertoire had slightly expanded beyond what I was originally hired to do. Shanisse, constantly frantic, would occasionally ask me to make some calls on her behalf to check facts, or request a press kit, or find out the status of a movie she was writing about.

'You sure are polite,' she said to me once, as she heard me on the phone with a studio publicist, starting the conversation with my customary: 'Good morning, sir. I wonder if you would be so kind as to . . .'

'We're the *Hollywood Insider*,' she reminded me. 'We're allowed to make demands. People should be bowing and scraping to get in good with us, not the other way around. So, honey, you make *them* beg!'

I knew what she meant, but couldn't.

Once the other writers and reporters saw how I was working with Shanisse, their own requests began pouring in. Aimee, the blonde nightclub reviewer who had 'had relations' on someone else's desk, started asking me to RSVP on her behalf to all the raves and opening parties she got invited to; according to Shanisse, Aimee was too junior to have her own assistant, so I became a *de facto* one. Roberto, a very genial researcher, originally from Rome, who liked to kiss his colleagues good morning, started asking me to deal with some of his personal business, like getting his change-of-address cards out when he moved house, or booking flights to Naples for his vacation. I knew that I wasn't obliged to be doing any of it, but he would call me '*bella*' and I would smile and blush and happily acquiesce to whatever he wanted. I knew Roberto was happy with me when he told me that he wished someone would find him a 'nice domesticated Asian wife too'.

These people, I knew, were all senior to me, and so had the right to tell me what to do. And beyond that still, because I helped them all out and never said no, eventually they all knew my name. I wasn't ever asked to join them for lunch, or even for a warm mid-morning beverage in the coffee room, but at least they said hello and asked me how my weekend was (without really stopping to hear my response). But it was good enough for me.

Mostly, I loved it – except for the one day when I spent forty-five minutes crying in the washroom and was sure I was about to lose my job. Joey, a photographer who was mean-spirited at the best of times, was expecting a package, which lay at the bottom of Deanna's trolley for two days, covered by the copies of *US Weekly* she wheeled around to read in her spare time. By the time she found it, Joey had raged on the phone with the person who had sent it, had turned over my desk twice, and was generally more foul-tempered than usual. So when Deanna handed it over to me, her usually pink and cheery face white with fear, I placed it pristinely atop the counter as if it had just arrived.

'*There* it is!' Joey yelled when he saw it. 'This was coming by messenger from Westwood, for Christ's sake! How the hell did it take two days to get here?'

'Sorry, Mr Joey,' I replied. 'I believe it got misdirected between the mail room and here. I'm not sure what happened,' I said, as Deanna hid behind her trolley in a corner.

'Well, *you're* supposed to be the go-to girl for this kind of thing, so I hold *you* responsible!' he bellowed, pointing a finger at me, while people stopped to watch. 'You'd better make damn sure this doesn't happen again!'

Deanna bought me a potted plant afterwards, herself almost in tears.

'I shouldn't have let you take the fall for that,' she said, her mascara clumping at the lashes. 'It was pretty cowardly of me. But that Joey has had it in for me for months, and I can't afford to lose this job. I'm so so so so sorry, and grateful,' she said.

'It's OK,' I replied, still smarting. 'Everything happens for a reason.'

12

The day that my life changed, I had been on the phone for ten minutes with a freelance writer who had called wondering which editor he should pitch an idea to about 'the recent trend of gay culture'. He wanted to explain his thoughts to me first, as if I had any say in any of this, using words like '*Zeitgeist*' and 'unrelenting cultural reprobation', as I continued to nod and say, 'Yes, of course, that sounds wonderful, let's see whom you can speak with.' I put him through to the features commissioning editor, sighed with relief that I no longer had to deal with him, and then picked up another line. It was Shanisse.

'Hi, there you are, so glad you answered,' she said, sounding frantic. She also sounded like she had been crying.

She asked me to put her on hold and go and look around her department to see if any of the other movie correspondents were in. 'I've been calling them on their direct lines, and nobody is picking up,' she said.

I went to check and, sure enough, it being close to lunchtime, the place was empty.

'Damn,' she said. 'Michael – you know, my boyfriend – and I were up fighting all night again, and I just got out of bed and I'm a mess,' she said, sniffling. 'I need to be at an interview in ten minutes. I'll never make it in time. That's why I was hoping one of the other reporters down there could do it for me.'

'I'm sorry to hear about you and your boyfriend,' I said. 'If you'd like me to reschedule the interview on your behalf, I'd be happy to.'

'You don't understand,' Shanisse said, sounding frustrated. 'I'm supposed to be interviewing Rex Hauser, and you don't change appointments with people like him. If I don't make it for the one fifteen slot, especially because of such a stupid reason, we lose our story. And if that happens, believe me, Lynette will fire me.'

I knew that Lynette was on a set visit in Tahiti. And even I had heard of Rex Hauser; he had won a Best Actor Oscar last year, and couldn't go anywhere with women screaming 'Sexy Rexy' at him.

'I wish I could help you, Shanisse,' I said. 'You sound really distraught. Just tell me what you'd like me to do.'

'I can't believe I'm going to say this,' she said, blowing her nose, 'but I guess I don't really have any choice . . . I think you need to go and do it for me.'

The receiver, literally, slipped out from under the crook of my neck where it was resting.

'*What?*' I exclaimed. 'Shanisse, this is me, Priya, the receptionist!'

'Look, all you have to do is grab the tape recorder on top of my desk, press record, and let him talk. He's promoting his new movie, *Constantinople*, so it's in his best interests to blab on about it. If you leave now, you'll be there in ten minutes, and you can be back before the end of your lunch hour. Please.'

She continued barking instructions – that Hauser always checked in at hotels under the name of his gardener, Miguel Gomez, and that's who I was supposed to ask for when I got there; that the press notes from the screening she had gone to the other night were also on her desk, and it would help if I read them quickly, but it wasn't really necessary.

'Shanisse, come on, I can't do this,' I said quietly. 'I have no right being in a place like that, talking to someone as famous as him. What if I say something stupid, or if I have no idea what he's talking about? I know nothing about this business. I'm just the receptionist. And anyway, I told you, my in-laws have forbidden me from doing any such thing.'

There was silence for a second, and then the sound of Shanisse blowing her nose again.

'Trust me, Priya, it's a no-brainer. You know, most people would kill for the opportunity to meet someone like Rex Hauser. You should be screaming with delight that I've asked you. And your family will never know about it – you don't have to tell them and how would they ever find out? It's just like you and the clothes. But listen, I don't have time to be standing here convincing you. If you don't get there, nobody will, and I'll most probably lose my job. It's your call.'

Now it was my turn to be silent.

Then I asked timorously, 'Where is this place?'

'The W.'

'W what?' I asked.

'The W Hotel! Jeez, Priya, you've lived in LA for months already. Don't tell me you don't know the W Hotel!'

'I don't, actually,' I said quietly. There was no reason I should be familiar with it; in my family, a treat was the $4.99 lunch special at the Tandoor Palace in Canoga Park.

'Look, just get going,' she said, impatient. 'I'll be back as soon as I can, and then I'll transcribe the notes from the tape and write it up. I'll even pay you.'

'I don't care about that,' I said. 'I hope you know what you're asking of me. I don't think you're doing the right thing, but if you really need me to go, then I'll go.'

Owing to some miracle of foresight on my part, I had brought my fake suede jacket – which looked remarkably real and quite stylish – and which I now threw on over my outfit. As my heart beat wildly beneath my embroidered teal top, I walked quickly to Shanisse's cubicle and pulled the press kit and tape recorder from the top of her desk, remembered to take a blank tape from the stationery closet, and rushed towards the elevator.

I backed out of my parking spot, almost rear-ending another car as I checked my make-up in the mirror, which was an annoyingly LA thing to do. I stopped for a second, told my heart to stop beating so fast, took a couple of deep breaths, checked my make-up again, and then cruised onto Wilshire Boulevard. Then I realized that I had absolutely no idea where the W was, and, still thinking what a ridiculous name that was for a hotel (why didn't they just call it the B? Or the Q? Or something self-explanatory like the Best & Beautiful Guesthouse, as was on our street in Delhi?) I called 411 from my mobile and got directions from a harried-sounding concierge there. It was, compared to everything else in LA, almost around the corner, so I was there in ten minutes. I went to a house phone and asked the operator to connect me to the room of Miguel Gomez. She sounded as if she was in on the secret, and did so immediately. Five seconds later, a deep voice came on the line.

'Yes?' he said.

'Good afternoon, Mr Hauser, sir,' I replied. 'I'm from *Hollywood Insider*.'

'Come on up,' he said, giving me his room number.

In the elevator, so small and dark that it reminded me of those manually operated ones that we had in India, butterflies whizzed around in my stomach as each floor brought me closer to what I was certain would be a disaster. I knocked on the door of his suite, and was stunned that he opened it himself. I remembered that Shanisse had said it would be just him, but didn't these people have butlers and a coterie of servants? What was a megastar like Rex Hauser doing opening a door?

He stood there, taller than I had imagined, dressed in jeans and a pale blue shirt, and extended his hand.

'Come on in,' he said. 'I'm Rex Hauser.'

'Hello, very nice to meet you,' I said, trembling.

'Sandy, my publicist, said to tell you she had a lunch engagement, but figured I was in good hands.' He led me into his suite, and I got a whiff of something on his breath – it smelled a bit like whisky, but that couldn't be possible: it was only lunchtime. The room was as dark as the elevator, and contained not a lot of furniture, and whatever was there was simple, in sober colours. I gathered this would be what they called 'minimalist chic' in this country, and it surprised me that someone in the league of Rex Hauser didn't want to surround himself in a more Sultan of Brunei-type environment: antique furniture, crystal chandeliers, gold statues – the kind of things that everyone I knew associated with wealth and luxury.

'How's Lynette?' he asked, folding his frame into a chair opposite me. 'I hear she's off on that war movie junket in Tahiti, right? Give her my best,' he said, not realizing that I had never even spoken to her.

Rex Hauser was staring at me, his eyes watery and glazed. He looked either as if he might just have woken up, or that he badly needed a nap.

'Well, Mr Hauser, as you know I'm here to talk to you about *Constantinople*,' I said nervously, hoping he would take the lead from there. I had glanced through the press notes as I had stopped at red lights and in elevators, but all I had gathered about the movie was that it was set in ancient Roman times and was about a corrupt emperor – played by the man in front of me – and the women in his life. And one woman in particular, a part given to Tamara Divan, who was the biggest actress in Hollywood.

I pressed the 'record' button on the tape recorder, and waited for him to start talking. The silence seemed endless and I was certain that he was wondering why such an incompetent had been sent to interview him.

'Hang on just a second,' he said. 'I need to get something.' He stood up and went to a cabinet against the wall, opened up the small glass door, and pulled out two miniature bottles of vodka.

'Would you like one?' he asked, holding one up.

'Thank you, no,' I replied, looking at my watch to make sure that it was, indeed, only one twenty in the afternoon, and perhaps not the most ideal time of day to be drinking hard liquor.

'Helps me relax,' he said, pouring the alcohol into a tumbler along with some orange juice, and stirring in ice. 'Are you sure you don't want one?'

'I'm certain, sir, thank you.'

'Call me Rex,' he said, downing the drink, and then quickly fixing another.

107

For the next twenty minutes, he stood propped up against the cabinet, and consumed not just those two vodkas, but a little bottle of gin too. He ripped open three packets of honey-glazed peanuts and flung those in his mouth while he drank and talked. His face was florid, his speech slurred, his eyes glazed. I was trying to listen and take notes as the tape recorder whirred away, but part of my brain was willing me to call someone; maybe Alcoholics Anonymous set up a satellite branch at this hotel every time Rex Hauser was in the building.

But I remained frozen in politeness. I had a job to do, and I was going to do it. For a while, Rex talked about the making of the movie, the grandness of the set, the big budget, the brilliant director. Then, as the gin mixed with the vodka, which apparently mixed with the whisky, he suddenly looked angry, and started sputtering out four-letter words about an unnamed woman. She was, he said, 'the cruelest and vilest female on the planet.

'Can't tell you how many times I came *this close*,' he said, holding up his thumb and forefinger half an inch apart, 'to wringing her skinny neck. *All those demands!* Her trailer had to be bigger than mine, her role more damn important. She would throw tantrums at least three times a day, screwing everything up. *I* was the star of the movie!' he screamed. 'She was only on it because I brought her on, and then she tried to wreck it every step of the way!'

He was talking about Tamara Divan, the actress who

had built her image on being a girl-next-door type: wholesome and humble. I leaned over and turned off the tape recorder; even listening to this seemed inappropriate – like overhearing someone else's private conversations. My grandmother used to tell me that anyone who did that would come back in their next life as a lizard.

God, what was I doing, remembering a silly Hindu superstition at a time like this?

Finally, Rex stopped speaking. It was almost as if he had run out of steam, like a roller coaster car that had reached the end of its track. He looked exhausted.

I put the tape recorder back in my bag, smiled congenially, and said: 'Excellent. That looks great, Mr Hauser, er, Rex. I think I have everything I need. Thank you so much for your time. Best of luck with the movie. I'm sure it'll do really well. OK, I'd better go,' I said, making towards the door. He thundered towards me, causing me to hold my breath in panic, but simply extended his hand, opened the door, and saw me out.

'Love to Lynette,' he said again, as I almost ran down the hallway.

13

In my car five minutes later, I sat behind the steering wheel, stunned. It was strangely exhilarating – the past hour had been the most exciting time I had had since getting married and moving to America; the frenzy of racing out of the office, making it to the hotel in time, knowing I was about to meet someone that even tribal folk in Zaire had heard of. Nothing is more memorable than when the day you thought you might have takes a different course and becomes something else entirely. I shook my head at the drama of it all, and went back to the office.

About an hour later, Shanisse rushed in, looking as if she had just completed a triathlon.

'How did everything go?' she asked me, anxiety printed on her face. 'Did you get there in time? Did the interview go OK?

'Um, yes, I did leave you a message earlier,' I said, handing over the tape recorder. 'He talked a lot about the movie. I'm sure you'll have enough information for your story. And how are you feeling, by the way? Did you and Michael patch things up?'

'Rex is great, isn't he?' Shanisse said, ignoring my question about her boyfriend. 'A real charmer. And *so* professional.'

'Actually, Shanisse, I need to tell you something,' I said, lowering my voice. 'He got a bit, well, drunk,' I said. 'Not a bit, actually. A lot drunk.'

Shanisse blinked at me.

'What? In broad daylight?' she asked.

I nodded. 'He was so drunk I don't think he knew what he was saying, and he was really, really nasty about Tamara Divan. Said she was the meanest, rudest and even the worst actress he had ever worked with.'

Suddenly, Shanisse was smiling. 'Do you know what you have here?' she asked. 'You've got gold. Gold! Not that *Hollywood Insider* would ever run anything like that – well, not without significantly toning it down and talking maybe a bit about "on-set rivalry". But you know we own that tabloid two floors down, the *Weekly Buzz*? Well, they'd *love* this! They get half their scoops from people here, who report the tidbits that we can't use, and pocket an easy five hundred dollars for it, and it's then attributed to some "source close to the star" so your name is never mentioned. That's all you'd have to do. Write a note to the news editor – I'll give you his email address – spelling out exactly what Hauser said about Divan, and they can probably use it for the next issue. They may even splash it all over the cover, to time it with the release of the movie.'

'Oh, I don't know, Shanisse. That doesn't seem quite right,' I said, fingering the gold loop in my ear. 'I don't think he knew what he was saying.'

'They usually don't,' she said. 'Look, often this kind of thing ends up working in their best interests. The *Weekly Buzz* has huge circulation, and it runs a story about high drama on the set between the two biggest stars, the movie comes out, and everyone wants to go and see it based on that. There's no such thing as bad publicity, you know?'

'I'll think about it,' I said, realizing that five hundred dollars would probably come in handy, what with my new wardrobe and all. 'But in the meantime, here are the notes. Take these, and if you need anything else, let me know.'

'Thanks, Priya. You're a star.'

It was close to the end of the day, and I thought I'd visit the ladies' room before making the long and most likely traffic-riddled drive home. It would also take a little longer than usual today, as my mother-in-law had called and asked if I could stop off at the Indian store near our home and pick up a packet of coriander powder for tonight's potato curry.

I wandered past Shanisse's desk, wondering if she had some last-minute queries. She was sitting at her computer, her back to me, typing out an email. I wouldn't ordinarily have looked, but the words 'Rex', 'Tamara', 'fiasco' and 'tantrums' flew out at me. She heard me behind her, and spun around in her swivel chair so fast I thought she might give herself whiplash.

'Oh, it's just you,' she said, relieved.

'I couldn't help noticing what you were doing, Shanisse,' I said quietly. 'To whom are you telling that story?'

'Oh, just sending a little snippet to the editor at the *Weekly Buzz*, like I said you should do. I figured you were either busy or shy, so I'm taking the liberty of doing it for you. It's easy money, and will get you in good with those people down there.'

'You know, Shanisse, I've been thinking about it and I really don't feel that comfortable. It seems exploitative and unnecessary. I don't know if he even meant any of it. People say stupid things when they're drunk,' I said, although I personally hadn't ever been drunk. I do remember, though, that Sanjay had had too much wine the day before our wedding, and said something about how his mother 'drove him *pagal*' – crazy. Maybe there was some truth in alcohol-induced mutterings after all.

'Look, he knew you were a reporter. What did he think? That you were just going to sit on that kind of stuff?' she asked logically.

'He was *drunk*,' I insisted. 'I doubt he was thinking anything. Please, just drop it. For now, anyway. OK?' I'm sure that on my grandmother's list of 'things guaranteed to blight one's karma into infinity', repeating malicious gossip came not far behind eavesdropping. Doing so, I recall her once telling me, would bring me back in my next life as a cockroach, which I thought was far worse than being a lizard.

At that second, I heard a commotion from down the hall, in the reception area. I heard a woman's voice say: 'I don't know her name' very loudly, and then *that voice* – the voice of Rex Hauser. It sounded tired, but it was his.

'Look, we didn't exactly exchange name-cards,' he was saying. 'She was petite, pretty, Indian, or Pakistani, or from somewhere like that. Her English was perfect. Fabulous accent, like out of some Merchant-Ivory film. Come on, you've got to know who I'm talking about.'

I suspected they were talking about me, so appeared in the foyer, and saw the man I had interviewed earlier, looking bleary-eyed but at least sober, and a plump, dark-haired woman by his side. They were talking to the Guatemalan cleaning woman, who was just about to begin her rounds, and who was trying to be helpful.

'There she is!' Rex said when he saw me, looking relieved. 'That's her!'

'Is there somewhere we can go and talk?' the dark-haired woman said to me officiously, holding me by the elbow.

I led them to a conference room down another hallway, which I knew would be empty at the end of the day. The woman introduced herself as Rex's publicist, Sandra Krugman, and we shut the door behind us.

'Nobody can hear us in here, right?' she asked, scanning the room as if looking for hidden cameras.

'For God's sake, Sandy, this is a magazine office, not bloody Langley,' Rex Hauser said.

'I wouldn't take that tone,' Sandra snipped back at him. 'You're in enough trouble already.'

Rex suddenly went quiet and contrite, and looked half the man I had met earlier today.

'How may I help you?' I asked them both.

'First, what's your name?' Sandra asked.

'Priya. Priya Sohni.'

'And how long have you worked here? How come we have never met? And what were you doing meeting with Mr Hauser today when I know that Shanisse Taylor was supposed to do the interview?'

Now *I* was scared. Shanisse didn't tell me that I could get into trouble for this.

'She wasn't able to make it so asked me to fill in at the last moment,' I said, trying not to lose my composure.

'Who do you work under?' Sandra asked. 'Who's your immediate boss? Lynette?'

My palms felt sweaty and my head was spinning. I was going to lose my job over this. But before I told them anything, I needed to hear what they wanted.

'I'll be happy to answer your questions,' I said. 'But I do need to get home now as my husband is waiting for me, so if there's something I can do for you, please do tell me what it is.' I was clutching the Durga pendant around my neck, like I always did when I felt tense or afraid. The words came out strong and steady, and I couldn't believe I was saying them.

Sandra covered her eyes with her hand, and shook her head, and then looked at me again.

'When you came to see Mr Hauser earlier today, he wasn't in the best state of mind,' she began, as if reciting something memorized. 'He may have said some things about his co-star that were, in fact, rather inaccurate. He has been under a lot of stress lately, and hasn't had a chance to unwind. You know, it's been one movie after another.' She paused, as I nodded my head and listened. 'He had taken some antihistamines before you got there, and that may have impaired his thought process. So that interview you did, well, much of it may be false,' she said, trying to stay calm.

'Oh Jesus, Sandy, let me take care of this,' Rex said, exasperated, turning his gaze towards me.

'Look, Prayer,' he said, mispronouncing my name so badly it was almost funny. 'I said some things earlier about Tamara that I probably shouldn't have. She's a great girl, actually. We mostly had a fine time working together. There were just a few things that happened. So I'm worried that maybe what I said might be taken out of context. All I'm asking you, Prayer, is that you don't use it. Please. I know stuff somehow ends up in that thing called *Buzz*, or whatever it is, and that all you journalists talk to one another and the word gets out. What I said about her, you know, the angry things, please, if that becomes public neither she nor I will ever get over the humiliation. I never know when I might work with her again, and I don't want this nastiness coming between us. Please. I hope you understand.'

He looked as if he was about to cry. Sandra was biting a fingernail nervously, her eyes never leaving my face.

'Look, what do you want? I'll give you anything,' Rex said, waving his finger at Sandra, who immediately reached into her bag and pulled out a chequebook.

'Cash? How much? Or would you prefer something else? Camera? DVD player?'

I was incredulous. The world's biggest movie star was not only trying to bribe me, but he was beginning to sound like a customs officer at Delhi airport, asking arrivals from Dubai what they had stashed away in their suitcases. For a second, I was tempted. To Mr Hauser, the loss of a few thousand dollars would be as grievous as spilling a cup of orange juice. To me, it could be a Hawaiian cruise for two. But extortion, according to my grandmother, would rate a return in a future life as a slug.

'Mr Hauser,' I said quietly, reverting to my previous formality with him, 'there is no need for any of this. I am aware of the stresses you are under. You didn't have to come all the way down here to explain yourself, or offer to pay me not to use that inappropriate material. I was never going to. As far as I am concerned not only is it forgotten, but it never even happened.'

Silence fell on the room, and the movie star and his publicist turned to look at one another, both visibly relieved. Rex smiled for the first time since he'd been here, stood up, came to my side of the table, and held out his hand. I rose to shake it, and instead, he put both his arms around me and hugged me. I was too shocked to hug him back, thinking only about how to extract my face out of his armpit.

'I knew I had a good feeling about you,' he said to me as they left the room. 'You're a star.'

It was the second time that day I had been called that.

14

By the time I told Shanisse what had just happened ('What? Rex Hauser came *here*? To see *you*?') and extracted a promise from her that nothing salacious would make it down to the *Weekly Buzz*, it was well after six. This was, so far, the latest I'd been here. I called my mother-in-law from the car to tell her I was running late, and she reminded me again to stop off and pick up the spices needed for dinner.

At the Indian store, I felt as if I was back at home in Delhi, where customer service in the arena of dry goods hasn't been invented yet. Here, the man refused to leave his place behind the cash register to show me where the coriander was.

'There!' he yelled out in Hindi, pointing somewhere behind my left shoulder. 'There! Behind you! No, a little more to your right!'

Ten minutes later, reeking of *masalas*, I emerged out of the store, got back into my car, and drove home. Outside,

I did a quick body-scan: flat sandals instead of my kitten-heeled mules and the oversized pants instead of the slender trousers I had had on all day. I wiped off the traces of lipstick that lingered on my mouth, sprinkled some *sindoor* down my hair, and put the key in the lock.

Dinner was almost ready, and I just had to stir and spice and then lay the table. As I ran upstairs to wash, I felt sad that I wouldn't be able to share with my family the details of the adventurous day I had just had. Most people, I would have thought, would *love* hearing about it.

But there was no way I could tell them. After all, what had happened today had been exactly what my father-in-law had predicted the night he told me I couldn't work as a journalist: not only did I go and meet a man alone in his hotel suite, but there *was* alcohol, *and* he had offered me some. Was my father-in-law some sort of prophet?

There was no need to say anything, nor alarm anyone. It was an out-of-the-ordinary day, and tomorrow I would be back behind my reception desk working a straight-forward nine thirty to five thirty, and being at everyone else's bidding.

After dinner, the dishes done and the kitchen clean, I settled down with my family to watch a Hindi film. My mother-in-law was unravelling a box of mint thins for dessert, and insisted I eat at least four. ('How will you make a baby if you're so skinny?' she said, causing me to hang my head in embarrassment.) My father-in-law was gently dozing off on the sofa, and Malini covered him with a blanket. I rested my head on Sanjay's shoulder, and smiled contentedly. His parents were difficult and demanding, but they had, in their own weird way, tried to welcome me. I was a part of their family – not necessarily celebrated or pampered or cosseted, but an average, accepted, equal (sort of) member of the clan. It was better than a lot of Hindu brides could ask for. My in-laws hadn't threatened to set me on fire, or beat me to a pulp, which was the kind of thing I used to read about in the 'Dear Aunty Popati' advice column that *Vivacious!* ran every month.

Compared to all those girls, I was being treated like a princess.

As we waited for the videotape to rewind, the television was playing an ad for *Constantinople*. Tamara Divan, with her buxom frame, flaxen hair and sharp blue eyes, loomed large on the screen.

'She's *very* beautiful, hah?' said my mother-in-law.

'Yeah, and where was I reading, maybe in *People*, that she does all this charity work,' Malini offered. 'She's meant to be a real angel.'

'Hah! No chance!' I said, without thinking. 'She's selfish and temperamental. A real diva! You should hear the stories . . .' I stopped, realizing I had said too much.

Everyone swung round to look at me, surprised.

'*Beti*, how do you know this?' my mother-in-law asked.

'Oh,' I said quickly, 'office gossip.'

Chores done, clothes changed, mascara applied, I made it to the office the next day, where a slim gift-wrapped box lay on my desk. It was so pretty I almost didn't have the heart to open it. The paper looked as if it was made from spun gold, and it was tied up with matching ribbons. A tiny card attached to it said: 'For what you did for me. Thank you. Love, Shanisse.'

I carefully unwrapped it, having decided to keep the paper for future use, and inside found a thin leather box. There, resting on bordeaux-coloured velvet was a bracelet so fine it felt like a strand of silk. I clasped it on my wrist, and went to find Shanisse.

She was sitting at her desk, going through a stack of mail, and gave me a big happy smile when I walked in.

'This is beautiful,' I said, showing her the gold bracelet shining on my wrist. 'Thank you so much. You really didn't have to. I was happy to help out.'

'I just wanted you to know that while this is a great place to work, it's not often that a girl can rely on someone. So thank you for dropping whatever you were doing and helping me out. And what an adventure it became too, huh?'

'Yes, but I don't think I'd want to go through that again anytime in a hurry. Anyway, I'd better get back to the phones. Lunch maybe, later?'

Right after Deanna left with the mid-morning deliveries, a uniformed messenger arrived. He had with him a floral arrangement so big it looked as if someone had carved out a huge chunk of the Brazilian rain forest and put it on a plane for California.

'I'm looking for someone named Prayer?' he asked.

'As in what you do in a church? Stupid name, right?' he whispered.

'That's me, actually,' I said, quickly dissipating the smile from his face. 'And it's not Prayer. It's Priya.'

'Whatever,' he said. 'Sign here.' He unloaded the orchard-on-a-trolley and left it on the floor next to me. There was a card attached, but I didn't need to look at it. I knew who it was from.

'Dear Prayer, I'm not surprised your parents named you after such a pious and selfless act. You are indeed these things. My "prayers" were answered with you. Rex.'

He was obviously back on the whisky when he wrote that, but I did find the sentiment rather touching. Sometime soon, however, it would be nice if Rex Hauser could get my name right.

The delivery inspired whoops of delight from everyone all day – especially because I had lied that it was from my husband.

'That's *so* romantic!' Deanna said, as she trundled by again. 'If it's not your birthday or anniversary, you must have done *something* good last night,' she giggled, as I blushed.

'So how did Hyde Park end up in our office?' Lou asked later that day. 'And what? Did he forget the koi pond?'

Shanisse, of course, knew the truth without having to be told. But even she was stunned by the extent of Rex Hauser's largesse.

'We've done huge front-page features on the guy, and

we've *never* seen anything like that,' she said. 'You must have *really* made an impression on the guy.'

As I sharpened pencils the following day – it doesn't matter how high-tech a company gets, pencils still have to be sharpened – a note arrived on my desk.

'Please come and see me during your lunch hour,' it said. The message was handwritten neatly on a small beige notecard with the words 'Crispin Bailey – Editor-in-Chief/Publisher' embossed across the top.

It must have been meant for someone else. I turned the envelope over to check again, and there it was: 'Ms Priya Sohni, Reception'.

Lou was walking by a few minutes later, and I intercepted him.

'Hi,' I said, showing him the card. 'Do you know what this is about?'

'No idea,' he said, his face blank. 'Mr Bailey's assistant called me to find out who you were and how to spell your name, but that's all I know. So he wants to see you, huh?'

'Yes. Why would he be asking for me? And which one is he, anyway? I don't think I've ever even seen him here.'

'He's one of the owners, and pretty much runs this operation. He's a real gentleman, despite his power. The reason you haven't seen him is because he's in executive offices, one floor up. If he's asking for you, I'd go.'

I couldn't concentrate for the rest of the morning.

Shanisse was out on assignment, so I was taking her calls together with those of Lynette, who was vacationing in Tahiti after the set visit. There were a million other things to do as well, but I somehow couldn't get focused. An endless number of possibilities whizzed around my head: that the editor-in-chief had found out that I had stepped in for Shanisse the other day, and was about to take me to task for it; that Rex Hauser had complained about me; that I wasn't allowed to be accepting gifts from interview subjects because of my low-level position here. It could be anything. But whatever it was, it couldn't be good.

At four minutes past one, I was the only person on my floor going upstairs instead of downstairs. I reached the suite of executive offices, manned by its own receptionist, and asked for Crispin Bailey. She buzzed me through, and I was met by a dapper, bespectacled man in a pin-striped suit who introduced himself as the editor's assistant, James St Clareau.

'Follow me,' he said, gliding down the corridor, making no sound against the plush carpet. He opened a set of doors, and there, behind a desk the size of Lithuania, sat my ultimate boss.

'Hello,' the man said, coming around his desk – which took about fifteen minutes. 'I'm Crispin Bailey. Thanks for stopping by. Please, sit.' His accent was English.

Speechless, I eased myself into a high-backed leather

chair that looked like it belonged in one of those gentlemen's clubs where pipes were smoked and harps played into the night.

'You must be wondering why I asked to see you,' he said. 'Please, don't look so frightened. I'm not going to fire you.'

I realized that my mouth had fallen open and I was hardly breathing, still too scared to say a word. Crispin Bailey was among the most elegant-looking men I had ever seen, like someone out of a James Bond movie, and one of those people whose age it was impossible to guess. He had steel-grey hair that had been neatly combed to one side, although a tiny cowlick at the front gave him a slightly aristocratic air. He was lean and muscular, and was dressed in immaculately cut navy trousers, a crisp white shirt and a striking silver and blue tie. A jacket hung from a coat rack near the island of mahogany he worked behind.

'You've been quite the busy bee,' he said, sitting on the edge of his desk. 'Tell me a bit about yourself, won't you?'

'Oh, right, sir,' I stammered. 'Um, I'm from India. Delhi, actually. Just moved to Los Angeles about six months ago after getting married. My husband has been here since he was a child. I joined this company three months ago.'

'Are you enjoying your work here?' he asked.

'Very much so, sir. It's a wonderful job.'

'Well, you've obviously been making an impression,' he said. 'Especially the other day. With Rex Hauser.'

My heart stopped for a millisecond. I tried to stay

calm; hadn't he just said that he wasn't going to fire me?

'Look, I know all about what happened,' he said. 'Ms Taylor, Lynette's sidekick, wasn't able to get there in time and asked you to fill in. Not a big deal, hardly a punishable offence. But what *I'm* impressed with is how you handled what happened thereafter.

'Sandra Krugman, Hauser's publicist, is a great friend of mine,' he continued. 'In fact, she's one of the most powerful people in Hollywood, believe it or not. The company she owns represents the biggest stars in the world; she personally looks after three of them, Rex being one. She called me yesterday and told me everything. It seems that what struck her most was not that you didn't accept what Rex was happily going to lavish on you, but the poise with which you handled it.'

My hands were shaking, and I found it very hard to contain the feeling of delight that was shimmying up and down my body. Nobody had ever used that word with me before.

'Anyhow, Sandra seems to have told everyone in her office and outside it that you are now the go-to girl at this magazine. Starting yesterday, I've been inundated with calls from publicists wanting to know how to get a hold of you, which department you worked in, who you reported to. Of course, I'd never heard of you. And then I find out that you're sitting there, right out in front, all on your own, answering phones all day.'

I shyly lowered my eyes as Mr Bailey returned to his chair, and creaked into it.

'So that's why I've called you up here, to ask you if you'd like to join our staff of reporters. From what I've heard, you'd be very good at it.'

I was still speechless, my mind digesting everything that was going on. Poise? Was it such a big deal? Hadn't I behaved the way that ordinary people behave?

'Oh, Mr Bailey. I don't know quite what to say. Thank you. But it's not like I am trained in journalism or anything, like I'm certain everyone else that works for you is. And I have absolutely no experience. And I'm from Delhi, which is not quite Los Angeles, and –'

He held up his hand, stopping me.

'I've never been a big fan of journalism degrees,' he said. 'Either someone has what it takes, or they don't. With you, I'd like to be given a chance to find out.

'Listen, Priya – am I pronouncing that correctly? – Rex Hauser made an observation to me yesterday that I think you should hear. He said the reason that he allowed himself to get somewhat inebriated and come out with whatever he came out with was because he felt comfortable with you. He said there was something in your manner that disarmed him. He felt comfortable. It's a rare thing to achieve in a star of his magnitude.'

For a second I closed my eyes, to fully grasp what was being asked of me.

'Can I ask you something, sir?' I said, opening them again, curious. 'How did *you* get into this business?'

Crispin Bailey's handsome face broke out into a

broad smile. 'You know the *Sun*?' he asked. 'The London tabloid?'

I sat still, having no idea.

'I was their chief gossip columnist, digging up all sorts of dirt with my bare hands. This was back in the seventies, of course, when gossip wasn't as politically incorrect as it is these days. I was so skuzzy that my nickname was Coyote. Can you believe that?'

I looked at his expensive suit and polished hair, and said no, I couldn't believe it. He certainly didn't look like a Coyote. A Jaguar, yes.

'I eventually ended up in America, and founded this company,' he said, opening his arms wide. 'It's a whole different system here. Studios almost dictate what we say about their movies and stars. It's a little infuriating sometimes, but we work within those confines. The first thing I learned as a Fleet Street intern is that if someone you've interviewed sends you flowers, you've done a bad job. But here, every day, we get dozens of flowers and gift baskets from people we write stories about. So I guess you could say that I went from Mr Obnoxious to Mr Obsequious in, what, two decades? But I'm a much better man for it – happier, healthier, able to sleep at night. Anyway, enough about me. What's your answer?'

My in-laws, their faces scowling and voices raised in irritation, flashed through my mind. They would never permit it, so I'd have to conceal it from them. If I were to do this, I'd be betraying them. And my husband. This job would become my other life. And when would I find

time for tile-grout cleaning? And defrosting the refrigerator? How could I possibly?

'When will I have time to do the laundry?' I asked,
unthinkingly.

'Sorry?' Crispin asked, looking straight at my face.
'Look, if I need to convince you then maybe you're not
the person for it. But I'll tell you one thing – it's a once-
in-a-lifetime opportunity, something that other people
would kill for. What's your answer?'

'Forgive me, sir, I'll have to think about it. But, in the
meantime, could you please tell Mr Hauser that it's Priya
– P-R-I-Y-A?'

15

I returned to my desk trembling. Everything always seemed to happen to me during my lunch hour.

Crispin had told me that he expected an answer 'by the close of business, tomorrow', making it all sound far too serious and officious. I buzzed Shanisse at her extension, and asked her to meet me in the coffee room when she had five minutes.

There, I filled her in on my conversation with our boss, fully expecting her to throw her arms around my neck and gleefully urge me to accept.

'That's insane!' she said instead, her face expressionless. 'I mean, Priya, please don't take this the wrong way,' (if there was one thing I always knew, it was that if somebody prefaced a comment with that, I could be certain that my feelings would undoubtedly be hurt) 'but what do you know about entertainment reporting?'

'I don't claim to know anything about it, but I feel so tremendously overwhelmed at being asked. Mr Bailey seems like a smart man, and maybe if he sees something in me, I should explore it, no?'

Shanisse remained stone-faced.

'What about all that stuff you've been feeding me about your family running your life? Doing this is bound to infuriate them. How long could you keep it quiet? Did you think of that?'

'Of course I have. I'm thinking of everything. I just wanted to know what *you* thought about it. I really respect your opinion. I consider you my only friend here, not just in this office, but in LA.'

She seemed to soften at that.

'It just really sucks,' she said. 'I slave away for years at crap magazines up and down the coast, and you show up here with no training, no experience and really bad clothes and get a job offer in three months. It ain't fair.'

'I can understand your feelings,' I said, suddenly grateful that my father had sent me on the Dale Carnegie course 'Winning Friends and Influencing People', which was big in Delhi a few years ago. 'None of this is supposed to hurt you. It just happened. Now, I have to make a decision.'

'Do what the hell you want,' Shanisse said, turning around and walking out of the room. 'But just wait until Lynette finds out.'

Apart from Shanisse, I had nobody else to talk to. Sparkle, one of my gym instructors, had always been pleasant and polite, and I thought for a second about dropping in to see her on my way home, but to her I was just one of a hundred other sweating and somewhat unfit bodies. She didn't even know my name.

I thought of calling one of my sisters, but this life that I had for the past few months, as well as the expanded and enriched version of it that I was tempted to explore, would mean nothing to them. Their lives were compact and content and filled with small helpings of grace, and that was enough for them. Surely I couldn't burden them with this. I worried, too, that they would start to see me as more and more of an outsider, someone no longer part of a once-cosy group.

After dinner that night, I indulged in one of my little habits and glanced at my horoscope in the local paper.

'You will have the opportunity to do something significant for yourself,' said Sammy the Seer. 'Do not turn it down.'

I smiled at the coincidence of the reading, and determined that it was probably just a reference to Shanisse's invitation to take me to get highlights in my hair.

But as I was thinking about going to bed, my mother-in-law was suddenly inspired to clean the chandelier in the living room that we never used. She fetched me a ladder, handed me a canister of glass cleaner and a cloth, and prepared to leave me to it.

'What? Now?' I asked her. 'Mummy, it's ten o'clock at night. Why do you want me to clean the chandelier now?'

'Because you are here, *beti*, and just sitting. Next week, my ladies' group is coming and we will be using that room, so you may as well do it now. Otherwise, you'll get busy-busy again.'

Malini was reclining on the couch flicking through *Elle* while Sanjay was microwaving popcorn in anticipation of a Steven Seagal movie he wanted to watch. Neither one of them offered to help me.

As I stood on top of the bright yellow ladder, a chamois cloth in one hand and a sliver of crystal in another, I decided that maybe Sammy had seen right.

By the middle of the next morning, Lou had already received instructions to transfer me to an office, one of the glass-enclosed ones that I had stared at when I first got here.

'You know, Lou, I'm happy to stay at reception until you find someone else,' I said, when he came by to congratulate me. 'You've been really kind to me, and I don't want to leave you stranded.'

'Don't be silly,' he replied. 'Mr Bailey wants you to start right away. And really, three months is considered a record in his company. Although I thought you'd last at least a year. In our department, we were taking bets.'

'So who won?' I asked.

'Hilda, would you believe? She said she knew the second she met you that you'd be on to bigger things in no time. She came the closest.'

136

We both laughed, and I repeated my offer to stay until he rehired.

'Nah, don't worry about it, honest,' he said. 'We've called the temp agency and they're sending someone over. By now, they know us *real* well.'

He told me I had to stop by his office to sign a new contract, one that would list my title as 'Entertainment Correspondent'. I realized I would be in the same category as Shanisse, which, now that I thought about it, was probably what had irritated her the most. She seemed happy to be my friend when I was hiding behind the front desk in a common space, but had evidently never imagined that she would be able to see all of me, sitting proudly in an independent office.

'Of course, your salary will be in keeping with your new position,' Lou said.

I peered down at the contract and gasped: overnight, I was going from earning forty thousand a year, to fifty-five thousand. I was certain that that was more than Sanjay made, and vowed to make sure that he would never find out. His ego would never recover.

By three that afternoon, I was seated in a small cubicle that had been vacated by a reporter who was fired when it was discovered that he was using the director contacts he was making at the *Hollywood Insider* to get his screenplay optioned.

'Just get settled in here,' Lou said. 'Someone will come along and talk to you about what you should be doing next.'

That someone was James St Clareau. His appearance on the floor stirred up even more chat than could usually be heard among the people around me; apparently, like Crispin Bailey, he rarely made it down here.

'So, how are you liking it so far?' he asked, pushing back his thick, curly hair from his slim face.

'Well, I haven't done anything,' I said. It was true. Since I was installed in that new office, I had checked my email about a hundred times; it had got to the point when that familiar, friendly America Online voice was snapping at me: 'You *Don't* Have Mail!'

James told me to expect my first assignment soon.

'As of yesterday, because of what Sandra Krugman has been saying about you, all the publicists have been looking for you. I'm sure they'll be calling. You'll get busy,' he said.

'Yes, but what should I be *doing*?' I asked. 'They call me, and then what?

James then asked me to follow him, led me into one of the small conference rooms, and shut the door.

'Mr Bailey probably should have discussed all this with you before, but I believe he was so excited to get you started,' he said. 'There's a hierarchy in place here, with Mr Bailey at the top. Then, as far as movies and related stories go, as I'm sure you know, Lynette Dove controls almost everything, and all the other movie corre-spondents report to her. But we're trying something new with you,' he explained, suddenly making me feel like a guinea pig about to be injected with an experimental drug. 'We've almost created this new position for you, independent of what everyone else is doing. Basically, you report to Mr Bailey. Your assignments will come from him, and if you want to pitch anything, you will do it to him directly. Lynette probably won't like it, but we'll take care of that. It's not your lookout.'

He paused for a second, allowing me to take it all in. 'Any questions?' he asked.

'I don't really understand,' I stammered. 'I know how good Ms Dove is at her job, and everything has been working well enough so far, so why am I now in a position to potentially complicate it all?'

'People in this town love Lynette,' James said. 'She's astoundingly good at her job, a thorough professional. When it comes to reporting facts about this industry and writing straightforward stories and interviews, she beats everybody, hands down. But,' he lowered his voice, 'we're launching a new element to the magazine, providing a more up-close-and-personal look at stars and their lives. People seem to be in the mood for warm and fuzzy these days. And Mr Bailey is under the impression that you are the girl to bring that in. Oh, and read these,' he said, reaching into a cabinet and pulling out a stack of magazines – *Vogue*, *Harper's*, *People*, *Daily Variety*, even a few tabloids.

'You'll need to make yourself familiar with names, movies, faces, fashion brands, all those otherwise meaningless details that make up our little universe here at the *Insider*. In this business, it's as much who you know as what you know – the latest trends, the hot soap stars about to land a breakthrough role. You'll need to read as much as you'll need to write. Is that clear to you?'

I nodded, filled with excitement – and determined to hide my fear. After all, wasn't this exactly what I had dreamed of doing?

16

Before leaving at the end of the day, I stopped by Shanisse's office but she told me she was 'on deadline' and couldn't speak. She had always had time for me before.

'Come on, Shanisse, please, we need to talk about this,' I said, almost pleading.

'There's nothing to discuss,' she said tersely. 'Well done on your promotion. I'm busy right now, so if you wouldn't mind . . .' she trailed off, her back to me the whole time.

I drove home chastened, instead of in the upbeat frame of mind I should have been in. At the gym, I clambered back into the loose pink linen trousers and the white polyester shirt with the shoulder pads that I was wearing this morning.

Judging by the cars in our driveway, 'the men', as they were called, were already home.

Inside, Sanjay was watching television while Malini was painting her nails at the dining table and my father-in-law napped upstairs. From the kitchen, I heard my mother-in-law summon me.

'Priyaaaa!' she called out, in that sing-song voice of hers. '*Idir ao! Roti banao!*' She was instructing me to roll out the dough for the *chapattis*, which would be the first of many tasks tonight. I wondered if she would still expect me to do all this if she knew that I was the new fifty-five-thousand-dollar earner and movie-star interviewer at a magazine.

Probably.

At the table, my father-in-law and Sanjay talked about a customer of theirs who hadn't paid for the last shipment of bags they had sent him. A supplier in India had let them down, plus a recent consignment of leather totes had arrived in purple when they should have been black.

'Do you know how hard it's going to be to sell purple bags?' Sanjay asked me. 'Maybe at Halloween, to go with some Barney the Dinosaur costumes or something. But until then, we're stuck with them.'

Evidently, I wasn't the only one who had had a bad, boring day.

'It's a very good thing that you are earning now,' my father-in-law said to me. 'Ordinarily, I wouldn't like to take anything from my daughter-in-law, but if business doesn't pick up soon, we might not have any choice.'

'Please, Papa, it's not a problem. My money is your money,' I said.

* * *

It was a bizarre feeling when I got to the office the next morning and the new receptionist, Sunshine, was handing *me* a message.

'Didn't you used to work at this desk, until, like *yesterday*?' she asked me. 'Wow, that must be a bit *Twilight Zone*, huh?'

The phone number of Sandra Krugman was written down on the slip of paper. I went into my office, and called her immediately.

'Priya, great to hear back from you! Congratulations on the new job. I knew you had it in you! How are you?' she said, much friendlier than I had remembered her that day.

'Very well, Ms Krugman. And you?' I enquired.

'Please, call me Sandy. All my friends do,' she said. Anyway, honey, listen, the reason I'm calling, and I know it's really short notice, is that my firm is hosting a table at a charity fund-raising luncheon today, and we'd love for you to be our guest. It starts at twelve thirty. Can you make it?'

'How delightful,' I said, trying not to sound excited. 'What's the charity?'

'What?' she asked.

'What's the charity?'

'Oh, um, hell of a good question and I'm damned if I can answer it. Multiple sclerosis, I think, or breast cancer. Something like that.'

'I appreciate the invite, but probably need to check. May I ring you back in a few moments?'

I immediately dialled James St Clareau's extension.

'Oh, hi, Priya. Settling in?'

'Yes, very well, thanks. I have a question. Sandra Krugman just called and invited me to a charity lunch that her firm has a table at. I thought it was very kind of her, but wanted to ask your permission to go?'

'That's *wonderful*, Priya,' he said. 'Of course you should take Sandy up on it. The Parkinson's disease annual research fund-raising luncheon is a major event in this town. Very hot ticket. Lynette usually goes, but she's still in Tahiti. If you've been invited by the head of the biggest publicity firm in town, that's really saying something. Absolutely, run along.'

'Well, what am I to do there?' I asked.

'Nothing,' James said. 'It's purely social. You'll probably meet loads of very important people, so make sure you take your new name-cards – you should have those by now, right? Just enjoy yourself.'

Fifty-five thousand dollars a year to go to lunch. I liked this job.

I called Sandy back and told her I'd be thrilled to attend.

'Glad to hear it,' she said. 'Your name will be at the door.'

A couple of hours later, I was on my way to the address on a Brentwood estate that Sandy had given me. I slipped in a CD of the soundtrack from the latest Bollywood film, and let my mind be transported back to Delhi. Lata Mangeshkar, India's greatest playback singer, sang of love in a way that made Celine Dion sound like one of the contestants on *Pop Idol*.

The luncheon was being hosted by Jane Jensen, the wife of one of Hollywood's most powerful directors. According to James, she was a struggling actress until he married her, installed her in a magnificent home, and made her an 'associate producer' on all his movies. Her new-found wealth, fame and numerous surgical enhancements had propelled her from 'Plain Jane', as she used to be called, to 'Vain Jane', her new sobriquet. James had also told me that the Jensens had recently revamped their home, and that it had been featured in last month's issue of *Architectural Digest*, and he suspected that opening it up to today's fund-raiser was a way of, basically, showing it off.

Just after twelve thirty, I pulled up outside a majestic home, built like a Tudor castle, its wrought-iron gates left open to accommodate the endless string of shiny cars that were arriving. I got out of my slightly weathered-looking Toyota – a hand-me-down from my husband – and felt a bit embarrassed when none of the valets wanted to take it. Finally, one came forward, looked me up and down, cast a disparaging glance towards the car, jumped in, and drove away. At least he wasn't going to take it on a joy ride, as he might have done had I been driving a Lamborghini.

At a linen-covered table outside the mahogany door

leading into the house, a trio of blondes sat with pages of lists of names in front of them. I proudly said my name and one of the woman indicated to me to go in.

Inside, Jane had taken the theme of the party, 'Berries in Summer', and squeezed every drop of juice out of it. The tablecloths were strawberry pink, the crockery a delectable shade of cranberry. Each table boasted a huge crystal bowl from which tumbled chunks of rouge-coloured fruit. Candles were as skinny as some of the women seated on the fuchsia chairs. Everywhere, perfumed ladies blew kisses to one another across the room and beamed dazzling smiles, their laughter sounding like water trickling from the top of the Trevi Fountain. Pink champagne was being poured into delicate flutes, and although I didn't drink, this looked so sparkly and pretty I had to at least hold a glass.

As I scanned the room for Sandy, a young woman with a nose-ring and the highest heels I had ever seen tottered up to me.

'So, who are you?' she asked, downing her glass of champagne.

'My name is Priya,' I said, taking her hand.

'Hi, I'm Avery. This is something, isn't it?' she asked, her long-lashed eyes absorbing everything that was going on.

'Yes, amazing, rather like a scene from Thackery's *Vanity Fair*,' I offered.

'Oh, really? Which issue? The one with Nicole Kidman on the cover?'

I laughed, and took a sip of the pink drink. These people were funny.

'So, are you in the industry?' she continued, shoving a satin clutch bag under her arm.

'Um, no. Not really.'

Without saying another word, Avery turned and walked away.

'Oh, bye,' I said, waving to her skinny, departing behind.

Finally, Sandy found me, and led me by the hand, like I was a child, to her table. She introduced me all around as 'the new movie correspondent at *Hollywood Insider*', which caused them all to gush with delight. My table-mates included a few women from Sandy's office, three journalists from other magazines and a young actress named Cassandra Lucas, whom I recognized from a new television show, *Trigger Happy*. She was, like everyone else here, astoundingly beautiful and so thin that I was scared to exhale in case I blew her away.

Every other seat in the room was crammed with women who looked as if they were wearing Chanel and had been born doing Pilates; Demi Moore was here, Rita Wilson there. Sandy pointed out the hostess, promising to introduce me later. For now, though, Jane Jensen was busy swanning through the room as if she were gliding on ice, kissing cheeks and tossing her head back in girlish laughter. She was in a sleek suede trouser suit the colour of a dusky rose, her long blonde hair pulled back from a perfect face, at the centre of which was the smallest nose in history.

'Wow, she almost doesn't look real,' I said to Sandy.

'Trust me, she isn't,' she said. 'Probably the only thing still real about Jane is her toenails, and even those I can't be sure about. You know that Carly Simon song "You're So Vain"? I'm sure she wrote it for Jane,' Sandy sniggered. 'Oh, by the way, Rex says hi,' she continued, breaking a piece of bread in half.

'That's kind,' I said to her, composed although I wanted to whoop with delight. 'Do pass on my best wishes as well.'

'So, Crispin tells me you're from India originally. How did you end up here?' Sandy asked.

By the time I had finished telling her the story of how Sanjay and I had met, and the traditional way in which we lived, everyone else at the table had stopped talking and was glommed on to my every word.

'A week? You knew him for a week? Are you insane?' the actress Cassandra Lucas said.

'It's probably the sanest way to do things,' I said. 'My father *thoroughly* checked him out. We had our astrological charts compared, and were told it was a match. He was my *naseeb*, my destiny,' I said, thrilled to have all the attention. 'Look, here's a picture.'

I fished out the one I always carried around, and the women passed it around the table, cooing as if he were an infant.

'*Aww*, you look so happy here,' said Katya, one of Sandy's colleagues. 'You look like you've known each other for ages.'

148

'So what does he think of your new job?' Sandy asked. 'He must be really proud of you.'

I had been chattering incessantly for the past twenty minutes and suddenly went quiet. I didn't want to tell the clever, accomplished, sophisticated women at this table that I was lying to my husband, that I was little better than an oppressed village bride who had to have a secret life for her sanity.

Before I had a chance to answer, Jane Jensen took the floor to give a speech, basking in all the attention.

Thank heavens for vanity.

17

Again, it was astonishing what can happen over a lunch hour.

By the time I got back to the office, very slightly buzzed from that one glass of champagne and still able to taste the blueberry sorbet that lingered on my tongue, I could hardly recognize my little cubicle.

When I had left a couple of hours ago, all I had on my desk was a small brass statue of Lord Ganesh, the Remover of Obstacles and therefore something that no business should be without, and a framed print of the Goddess Laxmi, who saw to it that prosperity followed in her wake, something that no person should be without.

By the time I returned, it looked as if someone had dumped the entire contents of the mail trolley onto my desk. There were large envelopes and small cards, Post-it notes and folders, press releases and goodie bags. Some things were addressed to me, a lot had my name scrawled on top of someone else's. I looked around and didn't know where to begin. I had never received that much stuff in one day in my life, not even in Delhi, and that was my *home*.

Just as I was thinking that, Deanna came up behind me.

'Lookie,' she said, pointing to everything, as if I were blind. 'Did you see? Hah, did ya?'

'I see,' I said. 'I'm stunned. What, just in the past couple of hours?'

'Listen, girl,' she said, lowering her voice. 'The word is out that you are Mr Bailey's new – what's that fancy foreign word – *potage*.'

I narrowed my eyes and looked at her. '*Potage* is French for soup,' I said. 'I think you mean protégée.'

'Yeah, that,' she said. 'That's what everyone around here is calling you. Anyway, want me to help you open anything? Maybe those little gift bags?'

'I'll take care of it,' I said, itching to unwrap what looked like T-shirts, key rings and stacks of CDs. This must be what Christmas felt like.

As I went through the pile in front of me – which included invitations to premieres, previews of upcoming releases, and shooting schedules of movies, the phone on my desk rang. It was the first call I had received in my new job that I was around to pick up.

'Hello, Priya Sohni,' I said, trying to sound professional.

'Oh hi, Priya, it's me,' a happy-sounding female voice said.

'Who is this please?' I asked.

'Me. Avery. We met at lunch today, remember? Before you went off to your table.'

I suddenly remembered: the nose-ring girl with the killer-Kilimanjaro heels.

'Oh, right, yes, hi,' I said, wondering why she was calling.

'You're probably wondering why I'm calling. Well, I found out after you left that you had just started work at the *Hollywood Insider*, and I was just *so* impressed by that, a young ethnic girl like you. I'm so sorry we didn't get a chance to talk more earlier, but I know you were anxious to meet your group,' she continued. 'So I was wondering if maybe you'd like to have lunch. I'd love to catch up.'

None of this was settling in my marginally champagne-soaked brain. A girl I didn't know and had exchanged maybe two sentences with was suggesting we 'catch up'. On what? The last twenty-four years?

'Oh, Avery, that's very kind of you. It's just that I literally am right now starting this job, and I have no idea what my schedule is going to be like,' I said truthfully. 'Maybe we can talk in a week or two when things are clearer?'

I could hear her bristle on the other end of the line, before she spoke again.

'Of course, I completely understand. I know how busy you probably are. But can I ask you something, while I have you on the phone? You know, I'm an actress. Your magazine does this weekly feature, where

153

they pick an up-and-coming star and photograph them, and *everyone* sees it and it usually leads to great roles and auditions and I've been trying to get into it for months . . . and I thought maybe you could help me. Please?'

'Avery, I would love to help you out on this, but I just started at this job yesterday and don't know who does what. I didn't even know about that feature,' I said. 'Why don't you leave it with me for a few days, and I'll see what I can find out, OK? Maybe I can put you in touch with the right person here.'

'OK,' she said, sounding grateful. 'I gotta tell you, you're real nice. You're the only person so far at *Hollywood Insider* that hasn't hung up on me.'

I put the phone down, looked at the mess around me, and realized that I was now sitting squarely in the middle of some of the neediest people on the planet, who evidently expected me to be at their beck and call.

And I wasn't even related to them.

Later, James called.

'Jane Jensen is typical Beverly Hills society queen, isn't she?' he asked. 'She'd be a good source for you to culti-vate because she knows how things work in this town and is fantastically well-connected. But do it on the phone,' he said, smiling. 'That woman has had so many chemicals put inside her she's liable to explode.

'Anyway, Mr Bailey has your first assignment for you. Can you talk a minute?'

Maia Mourtos had done something extraordinary. She had become a world-famous movie star when, just two years ago, she was serving *dolmas* and *souvlakia* at a Greek restaurant in Encino. She was an immigrant who studied until her English was faultless, and who went from waitress to aspiring actress and back again until she finally made it. And she was now getting raves in *Calling Home*, a lovely romantic comedy that Sanjay had taken me to see the other week.

Mr Bailey told me he wanted me to have lunch with Maia Mourtos. Once I got my heart started again, he told me that lunch would be at her old workplace, where she once dried dishes and swept floors before she started earning eleven million dollars a movie. He wanted me, he said, 'to take a trip down Memory Lane with perhaps the world's favourite Greek movie star.'

It was going to be me and her and food and wine and free-flowing conversation (or so we hoped). A photographer would come early and leave, and Maia and I would talk about how she got to where she was, and what she had learned along the way.

'Not a puff piece,' Mr Bailey said. 'We want a personal and intimate, warts-and-all look at a celebrated woman. Do you think you can handle it?'

It had been set up for the next day, not really giving me that much time to prepare.

But then I thought of something else very pressing: what would I wear? Could I really go out to lunch with Maia Mourtos in a forty-five-dollar ensemble?

But first, research. I remembered that I had been sent a press kit from a studio about one of Maia's upcoming films, and that it was hidden somewhere in the pile at my feet. I crouched down beneath my desk and started fumbling for it, before hearing someone come into my little office, and speak in a voice that sounded vaguely familiar.

'What the hell do you think you're doing?' the woman said.

'Oh, sorry, just one minute, please, I'm looking for something,' I replied, still under the desk.

'And beyond that, who *exactly* do you think you are?' she said sharply.

I stopped what I was doing to find that I was at the feet of Lynette Dove, which is probably precisely where she wanted me. I turned upwards, and noticed that the look of fury on her face didn't detract from her pretty tan and post-vacation glow.

'My name is Lynette Dove,' she said, her arms crossed in front of her.

'Yes, I know who you are, Ms Dove. I'm Priya Sohni,' I replied, now standing as well.

'I don't really care *what* your name is,' she said. 'All I know is that I go away for a week, and when I come back there's a new girl who is apparently allowed to go off and do whatever she pleases.'

'Oh, really? Who's that?' I asked.

'You!' she shouted, infuriated, pointing a finger in my face. 'Weren't you the *receptionist* here last week?' she sneered. 'So tell me, who did you have to sleep with to get this job?'

If I hadn't practised my *pranayama* this morning, I probably would burst into tears. But I pressed my knuckles down onto the desk, took a prolonged breath, and looked her in the eyes.

'I am very sorry you are so upset, Ms Dove,' I said quietly, rubbing my Durga pendant again. 'I neither slept with anyone nor even asked for this job. I was offered it, through some great good fortune that I will never be able to explain. Where I come from, we believe that God only knocks on your door once.'

She stared at me, her dark eyes smouldering like two nuggets of burning coal, her small mouth reminding me of a coiled-up elastic band.

'Don't give me any of that Hindi mumbo-jumbo,' she said. 'I run the movie end of this magazine, and it galls me that you were brought in without my say-so.'

'Ms Dove, I am fully aware of the high esteem in which people hold you. If anything, I intend to learn from you. You are the most important movie person at this magazine, and will continue to be so, long after I am gone.'

Lynette let her arms drop, and stepped back.

'All right then, as long as we have an understanding,' she said. 'I know that Crispin – who I think is losing his mind – said that you report to him, but I insist that you keep me informed as to what you are working on. That way, wires don't get crossed. Understood?'

Five minutes later, Shanisse stopped by to apologize for what she referred to as her 'pre-school behaviour' the other day.

'I guess I was just a bit jealous,' she said. 'I had to intern at second-rate magazines for years before I found this job, and you just land here and nab one. But I'm happy for you, really. It couldn't have happened to a nicer girl. Friends?' she asked, holding out her arms.

'Of course. Friends,' I said, hugging her.

As I crawled along in traffic on the way home, my head started to throb and I cursed under my breath when I realized I still had to get to the gym and change. Today was the busiest, most eventful and by far the most stressed-out day I had had, since, well, my wedding day. And at least at the end of that I hadn't had to go home and do housework.

I couldn't deal with fixing dinner tonight, or doing the laundry, or wiping down the basins. I was in the mood for hot soup and television and bed. It occurred to me then that my father-in-law had obviously had a point when he decreed that journalism would be a terrible career for me. How could I be there for that, and be there for them as well?

There was a letter waiting at home for me from my sister Roma, the second eldest, who had always preferred long chatty notes on prettily decorated Indian letter-writing paper to static- and echo-filled phone lines. It had happened again: she had won third prize in a raffle at a local fair, coming away with two train tickets to Bombay, which she said she intended to give to our parents. Last week, she enthused, she had submitted a handful of Coca-Cola bottle tops, under one of which was imprinted a special motif, and had been gifted with a radio in the shape of a cola can. Roma was always winning things.

What happened with Radha was a tragedy. With Roma, it was different.

By the time she was twelve, it was evident that finding her a husband would require nothing short of a miracle.

Not that there was anything wrong with Roma. My mother, who adored trilling our names and had given us nicknames, called her 'RrrroMantic Roma!'

Roma read Barbara Cartland novels and had memorized every word of *Love Story*. She was not quite as fair as Radha, not quite as feminine. But she was a lovely, happy girl, her hair in springy curls around a cheerful face.

But as she hit puberty, Roma shot up as tall as the

green and gangly stalks that lined the edge of our garden. By the time she was nineteen, Roma was six feet tall.

It was the last thing that anyone had anticipated. My parents, while commanding of presence in their own way, are not particularly tall. Nor were any of our grandparents.

So how Roma inherited that particular gene was a mystery. But there she stood regardless, towering over everyone, her face beaming with the hope of being accepted.

Finding a husband in India, as most girls who have ever tried it know, is dicey at best. Finding one when you are the size of a Harlem Globetrotter requires an act of God.

'Even if she wears sandals only, how to find a match for her?' wailed my grandmother.

Kaki was understandably concerned. There were proposals that had filtered through, but they were all rescinded when it became apparent that the boy in question would, if he was lucky, reach Roma's bellybutton.

'And it's not like she can become a model or anything,' Kaki continued. 'She's lovely-looking and all, but not the catwalk kind. Whatever will become of her?'

Roma, for her part, wasn't too fussed about any of it, convinced that the man intended for her would come forth sooner or later, shorter or taller. He would fall for her, and not be deterred by her longitude.

It was her romantic nature, thankfully, that kept her spirits as high as her head.

18

As I tried to sleep the night before my big interview, images of Maia Mourtos coursed through my subconscious. I got out of bed at three a.m., paced around the room, took a few deep breaths, and was startled when Sanjay sleepily asked me what the matter was.

'Oh, maybe a little indigestion,' I said to him, wishing desperately that I could tell him how nervous I was, and why.

He switched on the bedside lamp and blinked at the sudden brightness.

'Shall I get you something?' he asked. 'Some milk or something?'

'Thank you, no, I'll be fine. Just needed to stretch.'

'Good. I didn't want to go anyway.'

I got back into bed, and spent the rest of the night sitting upright, staring into the darkness, thinking of all the questions I would ask her – *should* ask her. I imagined the worst case – that she would see me for the incompetent that I knew I was, would clam up, not share anything, and then call Crispin and complain about me. That he would then send me back to my old reception desk, which, I decided, was not such a bad thing.

So even in the worst case, I would come out OK.

Awake but groggy the next morning, I was anxious to get to the office, and to cram in some preparation before my lunch with Maia Mourtos. Before I left, my mother-in-law reminded me that it was *raksha bhandan* – 'Brother's Day' – and insisted I come home this evening in time to celebrate.

Deanna was already dropping off some deliveries when I got in, and a studio publicist was on hold for me, calling to invite me on a three-day set visit for a movie being shot in Acapulco.

'We'll of course take care of everything,' she said. 'Flights, hotels, all your meals. We'd love to have you. If you'd like to take some time afterwards to vacation, we could arrange that too.'

'Thank you for asking,' I said, wishing I could say yes. 'But it's really hard for me to get away right now. Family obligations. Perhaps you could check with someone else in this department?'

Then I sent Lynette an email telling her about the Maia Mourtos assignment, and I noticed as I typed it that I was almost apologizing for the opportunity, wanting to downplay it, I suppose, as I did when talking to my sisters about my marriage. It wasn't my doing, really, that good things had happened to me.

So I was relieved when, a few minutes later, Lynette emailed back with a terse: 'Fine, go ahead.'

Maia's assistant called to tell me of a change of plan: instead of me meeting the movie star at the restaurant, she was going to come by and pick me up, and we'd drive over together.

'That way, you'll have more time to chat,' the assistant said. 'The limo will be in front of your building at noon. It's a black stretch.'

The thought of being in a limo was more exciting to me even than the lunch itself. I had seen them on the streets and in the movies, as long as trains, their windows blacked out and framed in lights, holding very important people on their way to very important places. I looked down at my outfit, which I knew wasn't limo-worthy, but it would have to do.

James called to see if everything was on schedule.

'Just think of it as a girlie lunch,' he said. 'It should be relaxing and enjoyable. That's where the most revealing stories come from. Oh, and in a couple of minutes I'm sending down your corporate credit card. Make sure you charge lunch to it, the tip as well.'

My own credit card. I had never even held one in my hands.

The hours seemed to pass slowly that morning and I suddenly felt the need to call someone so I could tell them that I was having lunch with Maia Mourtos. I would want to sound cavalier about it, shrug my shoulders as if it were no big deal; this was just what people did in this business.

A few minutes before heading downstairs, I went into the ladies' room to refresh my make-up, spritz on a little perfume, and brush my hair to bring back the lustre that gets taken away by fluorescent lights. I was in pale yellow and beige, with an embroidered shawl thrown over one shoulder and some old jewellery from Rajasthan that my mother had given me. Compared to everyone else, it wasn't particularly trendy, but it was the best that I could do.

Downstairs, I was hoping that someone I knew from my other life would see me step into a limo – even the teller at the bank that I went to, or the guy who came to clean our pool.

But at exactly noon – with neither bank-teller nor pool-cleaner around – a long black car slid up to the entrance of the building. A uniformed driver stepped out, asked me if I was Ms Sohni, and then opened the door for me.

I clambered inside as decorously as possible – not easy with an above-the-knee skirt and a shawl that kept getting tangled around my body – and plopped down on the soft, deep leather seat. On the other side of the car, which seemed like miles away, was one of the most beautiful women I had ever seen – and I came from a nation filled with them.

'Hello – Maia Mourtos,' she said in unaccented English, extending her hand. 'Delighted to meet you.'

She was one of those people often described as 'effortlessly chic' or a 'natural beauty'. Although I was certain she was wearing make-up, it had been so expertly applied that it seemed to caress her complexion. She had long, almost-black hair that was left loose, pulled gently to one side so it tumbled down her left shoulder. Long eyelashes that were obviously her own, a face that was entirely blemish-free; not a single mark, spot or wrinkle. She was dressed all in white: a pair of trousers snug around slender hips, a crisp white shirt tucked in. A simple beige leather belt was wound across her waist, with the same colour shoes on her feet. Sitting next to her was a large beige Hermès Kelly bag that I had seen in *In Style*, that I knew cost thousands of dollars and that even movie stars put their names on a list for.

'So I understand you've just started at the *Insider*, is that correct?' Maia asked, affixing her gaze right on my face, which made me feel supremely inadequate. Oh God, with everything that had happened, I hadn't waxed my upper lip in weeks. I was sitting here in the presence of perfect beauty, and I had a slim, but ever so noticeable moustache.

'Um, yes, just started the other day,' I said, self-consciously moving my fingers to my mouth, as if I could spend the rest of my time with her hiding behind my hands.

'Are you enjoying it?' she asked brightly.

'Oh yes, thanks very much,' I said.

This was pathetic. I was meant to be in charge of this situation, asking the questions, being charming and witty and delightful. But instead, I was so dazzled by this woman that I didn't know what to say. It was easier

165

with Rex Hauser the other day, because there was a movie involved that we could launch straight into. I had gone there with a specific goal. But this was different. It was meandering, open. It would involve me being attentive and intuitive and personable all at the same time, and I didn't think I was any of those things.

Lynette Dove should really be doing this.

'I loved you in *Calling Home*,' I said, sounding like a groupie. 'It's one of the best movies I've seen in ages.'

'Oh, I'm so glad,' she replied. 'I really enjoyed working on it. There were a few scenes set in Corfu, and that's where I'm from, so it was a treat to go back.'

'Yes, what was that like for you?' I said, fumbling in my handbag for a notebook and pen, before realizing to my utter horror that in my rush to get to the limo, I had forgotten to bring any journalistic supplies.

'Here,' Maia said, pulling out a notepad from a small leather container fixed into the seat. 'I always keep these handy, as I'm sometimes inspired and need to jot notes down,' which I think was star-speak for 'just in case I end up with an idiot like you'.

'Thank you so much,' I said. 'I apologize . . . now, you were saying about Corsica?'

'Corfu,' she said. 'Look, just relax and enjoy the ride. We are almost at the restaurant. We can talk more there.'

It appeared that every employee of the restaurant had told every single person in their email address books that

Maia Mourtos was going to be showing up at this Encino shopping mall today. By the time we rolled up to the restaurant, there must have been a hundred people standing outside, many of them waving photographs of the star and autograph books, many of them just waving.

'Oh my God,' I said, when I saw them all. 'Are we going to be mobbed? Now what?'

'Don't worry.' Maia rested her hand on mine. For a movie star, she sure was nice. 'I'm used to this. Jack, you know what to do,' she said to her driver.

Jack stepped out first, and I saw that he was bigger and beefier than I had thought. He obviously doubled as her bodyguard.

'Miss Mourtos is very happy to see you all here today,' he said, addressing the gathering. 'However, she is here on private business, and would be most grateful if you would respect that. She will sign a few autographs and pose for some pictures, but after that, she must be free to enter the restaurant with her guest.'

I felt famous by association, aware that people were peering through the car windows to see not just Maia, but who she was with.

Maia had just checked her make-up in a slim silver compact, put on her most brilliant smile, and stepped out of the car. The crowd started cheering, greeting her effusively in Greek, blowing air-kisses her way. As I stood pressed against the limo, she signed a few autographs for people closest to us, kissed two babies, hugged an elderly women dressed in black and posed for photographs.

Then, just as Jack had asked, the crowd parted and allowed Maia to pass and enter the restaurant, while I tagged along behind her. As I was about to catch up with her, a young girl tapped me on the shoulder, and thrust a piece of paper under my nose.

'Are you someone famous too?' she asked me brightly.

'Er, no,' I said. 'I'm with her.'

The restaurant was far more upscale than I had imagined. Its owner, a jolly-faced Greek, who was introduced to me as Anatole, looked as if he was about to burst when he saw Maia.

'My dear, gorgeous woman,' he said, hugging her. 'How long has it been? For me, far, far too long. How wonderful you look! And please, my apologies for that crowd out there. I told my staff to keep your visit today secret, but you know how excited they get.'

They talked warmly and excitedly for a few minutes, while I stood silently and observed. Everyone at the restaurant had turned to look at her, unable to turn away again.

'Come,' Anatole said. 'I have reserved a private room for you in the back.' Down a small corridor, he opened a door and showed us to our table, laid out with shiny silver cutlery, white candles and fresh flowers. A bottle of champagne had been left to chill in an ice bucket close by, while two waiters stood at military-style attention.

Maia cast her eyes across the room, and thanked Anatole.

'It's lovely,' she said. 'But, you know, I think I'd prefer

to sit outside where everyone else is. That's where I spent all those hours, and where my memories are. Is that OK?'

Anatole looked surprised, but told Maia, 'For you, anything.' He led us back to the main dining room, and installed us at a corner table, right by the window.

'At least here you will still be private,' he said, whispering to us. As we settled at our table, François, the photographer I was told to expect, arrived. He took some natural, candid shots of Maia – squeezing lime into her sparkling water, talking to Anatole, glancing at the menu – and then left.

She turned and looked at me expectantly, signalling that it was now OK for me to start asking questions. But after all the preparation and reading and dream-state planning, I hadn't a clue where to start.

Anatole came by and poured us each a glass of champagne – this drinking-at-lunch thing was beginning to become a habit, and I was certain that my mother-in-law would call me a 'shameful alcoholic cheap girl' if she could see me now. But I pushed her out of my head, settled into my seat and pulled out the notepad that Maia had given me. Before we each had even three sips of champagne, trolleys of food started arriving – a delicious cool yogurt that reminded me of *raita* but here was called *tzatsiki*, bowls of *taramasalata* and olives and fava beans. Fried potatoes and *spanakopita*, which I was scared to eat because of the high quotient of molar-snaring spinach, *moussaka*, which I *couldn't* eat because of the beef factor (I may be lying to my in-laws but I was still a good Hindu) and sizzling chicken *kababs*.

James had said to charge everything, but this meal was going to bankrupt Galaxy Holdings.

As we ate, Maia started talking, and I made notes, occasionally looking up to say 'hmm, yes,' and nod sympathetically. She talked about how nostalgic she felt being back in this restaurant after two years, seeing the boss who had given her a job when nobody else would because her English was so bad. She told me about how many times she had messed up the orders, and that Anatole had kept her around none the less. And that when the auditions started coming in, he would let her leave work and not cut her pay. She talked about living on restaurant leftovers, and in fear, and out of a small suitcase, from one low-rent eviction to another. She talked about dreaming not of stardom, but simply the freedom that came with acting, being on stage, delighting people.

'Do you know why I believe I have continued to succeed?' she asked me, voice soft, eyes lowered. 'Because not for one day since any of this started have I forgotten where I am from. Not a day has passed when I haven't whispered prayers of gratitude to the Greek gods for the magnificence of my life. So maybe I have Jack and the limo and the clothes and the Kelly bag,' she said laughing, 'but I also have the memory of the little girl who lives within me still, dying for a chance to be someone else.'

Tears were in my eyes as I took all this down, and I

didn't know if it was from what Maia was telling me, or the way in which she told it. Or maybe the soft and almost imperceptible sadness of my own life, and the fact that I too had obviously been dying for a chance to be someone else.

She hugged me in the car as we arrived back at my office. I was shocked to discover that it was already four.

'I can't believe I told you all that I did,' Maia said, as I was about to get out. 'I have never talked like this to a reporter before. But I feel confident in you, somehow. Use anything you wish.'

Upstairs, Shanisse came by my office as I started typing my notes into my computer.

'So, how did it go?' she asked.

'Yes, good. Very good. What a lovely lady,' I said.

'Yeah, everyone knows that Maia Mourtos has stayed pretty down-to-earth. She's a bit tight-lipped, though; anal about her privacy. I know we've never been able to get much out of her.'

'Oh, right,' I said. 'I think she was quite comfortable in her old work setting, so that helped. Anyway, I'd better ring James back. He's left a couple of messages.'

Crispin was apparently keen to learn what had happened.

'You were gone so long that I thought things either went very well or very badly,' he said. 'Which was it?'

'Very well, sir,' I said.

'Can you have your notes ready by the end of the day?'

'But, that's now,' I said, looking at my watch.

'Yes. And your point is?'

'It's no problem sir, I'll get going on it right away.'

Putting the key into the ignition a couple of hours later, it occurred to me that I had gone from the Valley to the city to the Valley to the city and back to the Valley again, all in less than twelve hours. It was a crazy commute once a day, but more than that was insanity. And after a heavy Mediterranean meal, it was also rather unpleasant.

I had called my mother-in-law and told her that I was going to be late because of a seminar at the office that I had to man the phones for, and she tut-tutted but then said, 'Fine, we'll wait for you.' Crispin had wanted to see my notes immediately, and then suggested we meet first thing in the morning and discuss how the feature would be shaped. But I wanted to impress him so much that I gave him more than just my notes; I almost crafted an entire story out of it, and even copied some of the phrases and descriptions I carried in my head from my *Vivacious!* reading days.

By the time I got home, Malini was dressed in a pretty white embroidered salwar kameez, and sitting on the couch waiting for me, Sanjay reading the paper next to her.

'She's here!' Sanjay announced when he heard me shut the door, and my father-in-law was hoisting himself up from his favourite armchair by the time I greeted them. My mother-in-law came out of the kitchen, holding a small round silver tray, on which was a *diya* with a tiny flame burning brightly in it.

Malini stood in front of her brother, holding a bracelet made from red and gold threads woven together, a tiny 'Om' symbol at its centre. With her other hand, she lifted up the *diya* by its handle, and circulated the small warm flame around Sanjay's smiling face. Then she dipped her finger into a tiny silver container of red powder, dabbed her brother's bowed forehead, and fed him a small chunk of cashew *mithai*. She tied the bracelet around his wrist, and he kissed her on the cheek and handed over an envelope containing money.

I, watching from the sidelines, couldn't help crying. The festival came at about the same time every year, a day when Indian men are honoured by their sisters. It was precisely because I had only sisters that I so much wanted to be a part of this. Back in Delhi, my sisters and I would tie the bracelet, the *raakhi*, on our male cousins. It wasn't quite as authentic as having a blood brother, but was certainly the next best thing.

'Did you have a good day?' Sanjay asked, ushering me to the dining-table. 'Come, sit. You must be hungry.'

19

Sunshine had left a message that Crispin Bailey wanted to see me as soon as I got in.

'Did he say what he wanted?' I asked her, nervous again.

'No, just that he got your notes and wants to talk to you.'

I took the lift upstairs, found James, and then went into Crispin's gargantuan office as James waited outside.

'Maia's publicist called just now,' Crispin said, motioning me to sit. 'Maia was raving, thought you were an absolute charm. Loved talking to you.'

'Oh, how great,' I said, happy. 'I really enjoyed it too.'

'But that's not the reason I asked you up here,' he said, his tone becoming serious. 'Thanks for your notes. I see you tried to frame a feature already, writing an intro and even an end,' he said, glancing down at a couple of sheets of paper that I recognized from my printer. Priya, I don't know quite how to put this. But what you've written, well, it's rather vapid and banal.'

Ah, a bad start. Definitely.

'I didn't expect something Pulitzer-prize winning, obviously, but this is, well, it's like a third-grade essay. The clichés – my darling, they are as predictable as Liz Hurley in Versace.'

I could feel the tears at the back of my throat. I didn't completely understand what he was trying to tell me, but I knew that he was disappointed, and that in itself hurt more than anything.

'Well, sir, it *is* only a first draft, and really more a sequence of thoughts and possibilities,' I said, deflated, my voice cracking. 'I didn't intend it to be a fit-for-publication article or anything.'

He looked down at the pages in front of him again, and closed his eyes.

'The *Insider* is a top-notch publication. Industry people read it, average people read it. Everybody reads it. And the writing has to be top notch. And let's face it, most people in this artistic community have the attention span of an amoeba. If they're not grabbed by the opening paragraph, they've turned the page. This doesn't grab. If anything, it's baffling.'

'I told you that I wasn't a trained journalist,' I said defensively, willing myself not to cry, but realizing it was too late. 'I don't have the skills. I shouldn't be doing this.'

'On the contrary, you *do* have the skills and you definitely should be doing this. You know how to draw information out of people, and that's a rare gift. I can see by these pages that Maia told you things that she has never discussed with anyone. That's pretty impressive. But all I'm saying to you is that once you have the material, you need to learn how to put it down in a way that's easy and pleasurable to read. And beyond that, your internal critic must always be at work. I'm sure that Maia Mourtos is a lovely woman, but it's not going to serve anyone to read about her in that nauseatingly effusive and shockingly simplistic manner,' he said, his harsh words like little darts pinging at my heart.

He slid the pages across the desk at me, and I picked them up.

'Read,' he said. 'Aloud.'

I cleared my throat and began reading.

'"Not only is Maia Mourtos an exquisite woman on the outside, but on the inside as well,"' I began. '"She has a heart of pure gold. She is a very charming lady. She kisses babies and hugs old people. Everyone knows and loves her. She leaves people breathless in her wake, at her God-given beauty and kindness. We went for lunch, and she told me some super-interesting things."' I still couldn't see what the problem was: I had once read an interview in *Vivacious!* about a former Miss India that was exactly like this.

'"Maia believes that to get, you have to give. So this extremely generous and lovely lady gives a lot. To charities and schools and orphanages. She might be a very huge movie star, but she cries at the sight of the homeless sleeping on the street, and – "'

177

Crispin cut me off.

'Sorry, I just can't hear any more,' he said. 'It's like a column for *Bleeding Heart Digest*. Do you see what I'm saying?'

I nodded, but I wasn't sure that I did. To me, truly, it was perfectly fine. Good, even. And certainly not vapid and banal.

Humiliated, I left his office, promising to try again. James saw the tears on my cheeks, and put his arm around me.

'You'll get there,' he said. 'Practice makes perfect. It was your first try, after all, and I'm sorry if Mr Bailey was hard on you. He probably expected much more and was disappointed.'

Returning to my floor, I ran into Lynette and Shanisse in the lift foyer, on their way out. Lynette caught a glimpse of the two pages I held in my hands, and burst into giggles – the first time I'd seen her smile – as if she were already familiar with the contents. Shanisse echoed Lynette's laughter, which made me sad. They saw my pink eyes and slightly swollen nose, and Shanisse asked me what the matter was, although the smirk on her face told me she already knew.

'Allergies,' I said, dabbing at my face with a Kleenex.

Sanjay snored beside me as I went through page after page, issue after issue, of the *Insider*. I had brought home twenty back copies, prompting questions from my in-

178

laws, which I side-stepped with a remark about an upcoming conference I had to be prepared for. My father-in-law looked puzzled, but said nothing. After dinner, once the rest of my chores were done and Sanjay had decided to go to bed, I sat in an armchair next to a tall floor lamp in the corner of our room, and read almost every feature in every issue. As I did so, I made pages of notes, comparing descriptions of celebrities and their lives, paying close attention to how the sentences were strung together, completely focused on the tone of what was being said. I read especially carefully everything that had Lynette's byline on the top.

Turning the last page of the last issue at four a.m., I glanced at my notes from the lunch again. I stood up, went to Sanjay's laptop, which lay resting in screen-saver mode on a corner desk, and started typing.

20

Jerry in IT helped me connect my husband's laptop to the printer on my desk, and left my office as I let the words whirr and whiz across the pages. When the printer went quiet, I picked up the four pages and read, reread and re-reread.

I called the receptionist upstairs to make sure that Mr Bailey was in his office, and then summoned the lift. When it opened for me, Shanisse stepped out.

'Hey,' she said. 'You're in early. You know, about yesterday, I'm sorry . . .'

'It's going up, right?' I asked, glancing at the floor indicator above the lift, realizing that I was unhappy with her. 'Look, I'd better jump in before the doors shut. Maybe we can talk later, yes?'

Upstairs, James looked mystified at my sudden appearance – this was the first time that I was here that I hadn't been 'beckoned', as he put it.

'Yes, but I'm really anxious to see Mr Bailey,' I said. 'I need to show him something.'

Crispin spent twelve silent minutes reading the pages I had given him. Then he stared at me, his face pensive.

'What a difference,' he said. 'Hard to believe it was written by the same person. Much, much better. I especially like this bit,' he said, pointing to a paragraph, preparing to read aloud. '"Mourtos now lives in seven thousand square feet of luxury, antique Persian rugs under her feet and custom-made chandeliers suspended overhead. 'But it's funny,' she said, suddenly growing wistful and gazing out the windows of the restaurant. 'It has become clear to me that it doesn't matter how well I live, or how well I think I live. It doesn't matter really that I am in a Beverly Hills mansion and not a walk-up in Compton. When I'm lonely, I'm lonely. And, truly, not even money can take that away.'" Well done, Priya.' Crispin placed the papers back down on his desk. 'It needs a bit of editing, but I think you're on the right track. We'll make a celebrity reporter out of you yet.'

Thrilled, I went back to my desk, hugged Deanna when she came by, and gave Sunshine a sweatshirt that one of the studios had sent me to promote an up-coming film. I was in such a great mood that when Avery called again – the fifteenth time that week – I let her talk for a full eight minutes before hanging up.

I felt like celebrating.

When I called James at three and asked if I could leave early, he checked with Crispin and said fine.

'Don't make it a habit, but if you want to take the rest of the day off, you can,' he said. 'And again, Priya, congratulations. I read the piece, and it's such an improvement.'

It was a thrill being able to drive home well before rush hour. When I got there, Malini and my mother-in-law were surprised to see me, but were pleased because I could get dinner started early.

'Not tonight,' I said to my mother-in-law, who frowned and appeared to be wondering if I was going to be the renegade wife who would never boil another beet again. 'Let's do something different. There's a wonderful restaurant near my office that everyone goes to. We're going there to celebrate.'

'Celebrate what, *beti*?' my mother-in-law asked.

'My job,' I said. 'I got a raise.'

'So soon?' Malini said, envy lurking in her eyes. 'You've hardly been working there a few months.'

'Yes, but it seems they're happy with me, so they gave me a small raise. Not much, but it's nice none the less.'

'How much?' asked my mother-in-law, ever the cash queen.

'A few thousand,' I lied, watching as her brain kicked into dollar-rupee conversion mode. 'So we're going out.'

James had called and got us in, as there was no way I'd be able to get a table at Spago on my own with four hours' notice. Malini phoned Sanjay at the office and suggested he and my father-in-law come home early as well. At seven p.m., my mother-in-law, Malini and I were all draped in saris, 'the men' in smart trousers, shirts and jackets.

As we approached the restaurant, I pointed out the building that housed my office.

'See, there, that's where I work,' I said proudly. 'Nice, no?'

'It looks nice on the outside,' my mother-in-law said. 'Maybe next time we're around here, we'll drop in and see it.' It was easy to ignore her: the last time my in-laws had made it to Beverly Hills was for a wedding, five years earlier. Sanjay occasionally came to see customers in West Los Angeles, but the Valley, where we lived, might as well have been in another state.

We left the car with the valet, and proudly walked in, straight through the restaurant to the courtyard at the centre, a sprinkling of lights in the trees overhead. Conversations around us were lively, waiters busy, everyone looking to spot someone else. We were shown to our table, and the *maître d'* personally came up to greet us.

'Welcome to Spago. Have a wonderful evening, and do let me know if there's anything you need.'

'*Aarey, wah!*' my mother-in-law said loudly. 'They're treating you like a big shot. So nice!'

Wine lists were offered, and hurriedly taken away when my mother-in-law loudly announced that 'we are not drinking type of people here'. When the menus arrived, my father-in-law almost spat his ice-water out.

'*Hai Ram!*' he said, Hindi for 'good golly'. 'Twenty-five dollars for salmon! Are they mad? Come, let's leave. For that I can buy a big tub of fish and chips and we can all eat,' he said.

'Papa, relax,' I said. 'Just order what you want and don't worry about it. It's a special occasion, OK?'

'OK, but main course only. No appetizer, no dessert,' he said, returning to the menu.

My mother-in-law was squinting through her glasses, looking perplexed, before closing the menu and putting it down on the table.

'Have you decided, Ma?' I asked.

'No. I don't know what all those things are,' she said.

She lifted up the menu again, and pointed to 'crème fraîche', 'fennel', 'radicchio' and 'galangal'.

'Even the pizzas are fancy here,' she said. 'What if I just want tomato and cheese?'

We spent twenty minutes conferring with the *maître d*' ('I have a belching problem, can you suggest something?' my father-in-law asked) until everyone seemed happy with their choices, and we could all relax and enjoy the trickling of the water from the fountain next to us, and the scent of oranges and lemons from the tall trees in our midst. It was a perfect night to be outside.

'Hi,' I heard someone addressing me, forcing me to lower my head so quickly that my upper teeth clamped on top of my lower ones, trapping my tongue in between.

Rex Hauser was standing right in front of me.

'Nice to see you again, Priya,' he said, finally getting my name right. 'And this must be your lovely family.'

My mother-in-law looked like she was about to faint in her soup while Malini's mouth was so wide I could have lodged a swizzle stick in it. Sanjay and my father-in-law gazed at Rex Hauser, and then at me, and then back at him.

'Oh yes,' I blurted out, providing introductions all around, as if we were executives sitting round a table at DreamWorks.

Rex nodded politely at everyone, threw a huge smile my way, and said he'd better get back to his table. 'Just wanted to come and say hello,' he finished. 'Enjoy your meal.'

My eyes followed him back to his table where he was dining with . . . Tamara Divan. He whispered something to her, and she waved at me, while he kissed her bare shoulder. No wonder he was so determined not to have any of his rantings published.

'Oh my God! That's so completely amazing!' Malini said, in typical LA understatement. 'Just wait till I tell all my friends that you know Rex Hauser *and* Tamara Divan. They'll *flip*!' and she pulled out her mobile.

'Not now, *beti*,' her father instructed, before turning to look at me.

'Priya, how do you know this famous movie star gentleman?' he asked, a stern expression on his face.

'Papa, he has come into the office to see the editors. I met him there when he was waiting in reception. I gave him coffee. I suppose he just remembered me,' I said, feeling a little guilty.

'But that's something he remembered your name, hah?' my mother-in-law asked. 'Must be a very smart man.'

'Yes, Mummy. He's very smart.'

When I asked for the bill, the *maître d'* informed me, 'Mr Hauser has taken care of it.'

My father-in-law cheered, and then said: 'If I had known he was going to do that, I would have ordered dessert.'

21

Arabella Tomas had made it to the twenty-million-dollar club at least four movies ago. She and only three other women in Hollywood collected that kind of a fee for acting, and she was, naturally, very proud of it.

But despite Arabella's growing collection of Golden Globes and Academy Awards, and a string of nominations longer than her skinny arm, there was something that Arabella just couldn't get right. That was, as she called it, 'the marriage thing'.

She had dumped and been dumped numerous times, and in the most astounding of ways, all of which had been chronicled by the *Insider* as well as every other publication in town. The gist of the stories was always the same: why couldn't someone this beautiful, this talented, this *thin*, get it together to keep a boyfriend for more than a month?

Then, seven months ago, Arabella had done better than that: she had not just found a boyfriend, she had eloped with him. Finally, she was a Happily Married Woman, at last able to escape the curse of endless emotional dramas.

Now, however, the rumours were starting up again. 'Cracks in the Marriage!' screamed the headlines. 'Friends Say It's Almost Over!'

Which is why I was sitting here, in Arabella Tomas's living room, on a breezy Wednesday morning.

Her publicist had called a week earlier, telling Crispin that Arabella 'wanted to set the record straight about her personal life', and she had chosen me to do it with.

'Who's that new girl you've got down there, the one that everyone seems to like talking to? Peru or Prism or something?' James told me the publicist had asked.

Now, I had already been waiting fifteen minutes, and there was still no sign of the woman. I pulled out the novel I always carried around in my bag, although I was far too nervous to concentrate; I was sitting on the brown suede couch of the most famous actress in the world, about to talk to her about the most personal subject in *her* world.

Photographs of her with her husband – a boyishly handsome man named Bryce, whom she had met when he was the set designer on a movie she had starred in – were everywhere. They looked profoundly happy in their widely ranging life – riding horses in leafy forests, lying together on sandy beaches, arriving at a premiere together. These were snapshots of her emotional terrain, when she and he could go from opening-night gloss to 'show me your cellulite', and still look joyful.

That was a clever observation, I thought, and jotted it down.

Finally, Arabella appeared.

'Hi, thanks so much for coming,' she said. 'Did anyone offer you something to drink?'

'I'm fine, Ms Tomas, thank you,' I said, smiling.

She sat across from me in a beige leather armchair, and crossed her long, jeans-clad legs. She was wearing pointy-toed boots and a turtle-neck sweater, evidently to combat the freezing air-conditioned temperatures in this room. Didn't movie stars care about electricity bills?

Crispin had suggested that I break the ice by talking to her about her latest movie, a stylish crime caper, and what she planned to do next. She answered my questions politely and amiably, although I could tell that her mind was elsewhere.

'My next film is to be shot in Melbourne,' she said, 'but I'm going to have to work that out with Bryce. It's hard, being apart for that long.'

I knew that that was my cue.

'So, tell me, every day another magazine publishes the rumour that you and Bryce can't make it work. How does that make you feel? And, more importantly, is there any truth to any of this?'

Her pretty face went blank, her mouth turning into a grimace.

'You know, I don't think this is such a good idea,' she said, starting to rise from her chair. 'I really don't feel comfortable discussing this. It was my publicist's idea and I went along with it, but now . . .'

She stood up, and so did I.

'I'm sorry you feel that way,' I said. 'Of course, if you're not comfortable, I don't want to force you . . .'

She frowned, and peered at me through her narrow spectacles.

'I just don't see how you would possibly understand,' she said. 'Haven't you just started at the magazine? And aren't you new to LA anyway?'

'Yes, but please don't hold that against me,' I said. 'They would not have sent me if I knew nothing. But, if you'd rather I go . . .' I said, reaching for my bag.

'No, wait. That's rude of me. Sit. At least have a cup of tea.'

We both sat in silence, unsure of where to go next with this. I didn't want to return to the office with no story – especially as Crispin wanted to use this for next week's cover – but I couldn't force someone to speak to me. Shanisse had told me that when she was a trainee at another entertainment magazine in town, she would shove microphones under the faces of interview subjects until they threatened lawsuits.

'Being soft ain't gonna get you anywhere,' she had said. 'These people wanted to be famous, so then they deserve all the intrusion they get.'

If I left now this assignment would be a failure. Somehow I had to get Arabella to open up, and not regret doing so.

'Are you into Bollywood?' I asked her suddenly, not

knowing where the question came from. 'Do you like Hindi movies?'

'I've seen a couple, yeah,' she said. 'They're kinda fun, although a bit unrealistic.'

'People outside India think that they are all fantasy, and that they don't mirror real life. But they do. One of the best ones ever made is about a beautiful girl whose soul mate dies the night before their wedding. Isn't that tragic? But that's what happened to my sister.'

I told Arabella the story of Radha and Nishant, how my sister was convinced that everyone only had one love, one *naseeb*, and that she would never find another. By the time I was done, Arabella had tears stretching down her face. It was so sudden that I didn't have time to reach for the packet of scented Kleenex I always kept in my purse, right next to the novel. She had literally gone from semi-smiling movie star standoffishness to bawling emotional wreck in under fifteen seconds. A record, I thought, even in Hollywood.

'Sorry,' she stammered. 'That's such a *sad* story. I guess I should be grateful. My problems are nothing in comparison.'

I waited before I picked up my pen and notepad again. This was all about timing.

'It's just that . . . well, it's been *so* difficult. Some days, I don't know what to do,' she paused. 'Do you have to write all this down?'

'Not at all,' I said, placing the notepad down on the coffee table in front of me.

'So we can just talk, right?' she asked, wiping away tears with a handkerchief she fished out from her pocket.

'Yes, we can just talk.'

An hour later, I knew more about Arabella and Bryce than probably their own families did; about his insecurity at her massive fame and fortune, her fear that she would lose him as a result of it. He kept throwing in her face that she had 'married down', and, when she got really, really angry with him, she would scream at him that yes, indeed, she had. Doors slammed, things were thrown, it was mayhem and madness all the time. It made me uncomfortable to hear it, as if she was confiding in me by default, because there was nobody else around.

After all, she didn't even know my name.

'Look, I'm sorry. I know you came here to get a story, to set the record straight. But I don't know what that story is. I'm as confused as anyone,' she said, taking off her glasses, rubbing her large brown eyes, and suddenly looking fatigued.

'We don't have to do this right now,' I repeated, even though I had spent an hour listening. 'I can always come back when things are clearer in your head. I wouldn't want you to say anything to me that you regret. I do have a deadline but I'll tell my editor something. Don't worry.'

'No, I don't want you to get in trouble for this,' she continued. 'We'll talk – officially now. I'll tell you the truth, just not *all* of it. Is that OK?'

Arabella offered me a watered-down version of her relationship tangles and her insights into the stresses of keeping a Hollywood marriage together. She was a movie star with a public counting on her, and she had to stay upbeat. Yes, they were having problems, but which married couple didn't? And yes, they were committed to one another and would stay together no matter what. I knew she didn't believe what she was saying, but I wrote it down none the less.

I had been sitting there for almost two hours, when Arabella finally noticed something about me.

'How long have you been married?' she asked, pointing to my wedding band.

'About six months,' I replied. 'I guess I'm, like you, a newlywed still.'

'And how are you enjoying it?'

'Yes, it's good,' I replied, realizing nobody except Radha had asked me that before. 'But you must understand, I don't expect too much from it. It is what it is.'

She looked puzzled.

'That doesn't sound very enthusiastic,' she said. 'Especially if you're still supposed to be in the honeymoon phase.'

'I didn't really know my husband when we got married, so we are still in the process of discovering each other. Some days, it is fine. Other days, I feel like I want to leave him,' I said, stunning myself with the bitterness of my words. 'He is completely under the thumb of his parents, and I suffer the consequences of that. I live with them, and it's not always easy.' I told her about my daily and nightly domestic duties, and she looked astonished.

'My God, *so* conservative!' she said, suddenly brightening that she wasn't the only one suffering in silence. 'If I were you, I'd leave.'

'Some days I feel like I want to,' I said. 'But I can't. Because the only thing worse than being a single woman in India is being a divorced one. And I know, somewhere in my heart, that Sanjay and I will make it. We will learn to fully love one another, and he will come to respect me, and we will make it.'

We heard a grandfather clock strike twelve in an outside room.

'I was going to get some lunch brought in,' she said. 'Would you care to stay and join me?'

As any Hindu bride knows, the beginning of married life is always bittersweet. There is the hope, held in the hearts of the parents of a newlywed woman, of a ravishing life ahead, one filled with the sweet voices of children and the endless falling of golden coins from the heavens.

But then there also is the final separation that comes between mother and daughter.

My mother may have whispered to me that I could

run home to them any time, but I was never going to do that. It was one thing to live in America, but it was another to live like an American – to run and hide and fight and leave.

In America, there is no shame in divorce. In India, there is no shame in living in marital misery.

Somehow, I was going to find *my* place.

I told Arabella that as I stood on her doorstep and she shook my hand goodbye. I wished her luck in her marriage, and she wished me the same in mine.

22

The 'lunch with Maia Mourtos' piece came out that week, and I was so thrilled I wanted to frame it. I would display it proudly in my office where nobody would ever see it. She sent me a single orchid in a terracotta pot, accompanied by a handwritten note of thanks, and even called me the following day asking if we could have tea sometime.

'Pencil it in,' she trilled, as my hand trembled atop my Filofax.

I had asked Crispin not to use my real name, which had confounded him. I was pretty sure that my in-laws would probably never pick up a copy of the *Hollywood Insider* – my mother-in-law had enough trouble keeping up with her subscription of Bollywood's *Stardust* – but Malini spent enough time in hair salons and manicure shops and I was certain she'd be leafing through a copy somewhere.

'Most people would do anything to see their name in a magazine like this,' he had said. 'What's going on?'

'Oh, it's a *really* long story, Mr Bailey,' I said to him. 'I'm sure you don't want to hear it. It's like a bad Hindi soap opera. If I start telling you, we'll never get out of here.'

That's all I needed to say; men like Crispin Bailey weren't inclined to hang around and listen to endless sagas about subcontinental family dysfunction.

'Fine, fine, whatever you want, your loss then,' he said. 'What shall we go with instead? Any ideas?'

We tossed a few pseudonyms around, but came up blank. Then, the day before the magazine was going to press, Crispin came up with it.

'P.S.,' he said. 'Short and simple. And it has that gossipy, insider-y feeling. It will also keep people guessing who you are. What do you think?'

As long as my in-laws didn't figure it out, I didn't really care.

My mother-in-law, though, was thrilled at the little gifts I would bring home – the baseball caps and pen-stands and other premiums that studios lavished on journalists.

'*Wah wah!*' she would say, rummaging through yet another goodie bag. 'Again you got something? Those people in your office are *so* nice to give you all these things they don't want. We can definitely use them,' she said, placing a pair of Terminator-style sunglasses over her eyes and looking around the room. 'We can start collecting now for Malini's wedding, God willing, when-ever that happens. These all will make *vunderful* gifts for when we go back to India. Why spend money when we get these things for free?'

She had a point, but I did have to laugh when I thought of Balram, the lift-boy in my father's office building in Delhi, sporting an oversized *Spiderman* sweatshirt.

I was fine tuning the Arabella Tomas story, trying to think of another way to say 'million-dollar smile', when my phone rang.

'Hey, Priya, some people here in reception to see you,' Sunshine announced. 'Cute guy,' she murmured.

Curious, I stepped out from behind my desk and walked out to the main foyer. After Rex Hauser, nobody else had ever dropped in unannounced to see me. And certainly nobody cute.

Seated on the couch in reception were Sanjay and Malini, and my in-laws. They looked at me in silence and confusion, taking in my black denim jeans, Chinese-style top and high heels. I could tell that, for a second, they didn't recognize me, convinced that Sunshine had sent out the wrong person.

'Priya, what is this?' my mother-in-law asked, as always, the first to speak. 'Whose clothes are these?' She stood up, to be followed by the rest of the clan. 'We were passing by, Sanjay was going to meet a customer, we thought we would all come to surprise you. But what are you wearing?' she asked, concern growing in her eyes.

'Oh, these, um . . .' I started, feeling my body turn hot with shame.

'Fab top!' Malini exclaimed, fingering the silk. 'Love the black and red combo. Where'd ya get it?'

'And where is your *sindoor*?' Sanjay asked, looking at my hair parting. 'It's gone! It was there this morning!' he exclaimed, alarmed, as if wiping away a line of red powder was equal to erasing his presence from my life.

'Priya's been *so* helpful,' Sunshine said suddenly. I had forgotten she was even there, seated behind my old desk, taking in what could have been a scene from a bad sitcom. 'We're doing a photo shoot with an actress and the clothes just arrived from the designer, and we thought they were the wrong size,' Sunshine continued. 'Priya was trying them on for us, and I'm manning the desk while she's at it. She's really such a trooper.' I recalled that Sunshine had told me she was taking improvisation classes, and she was obviously learning a lot.

'Yes, that's right,' I said, looking over at my family and praying that they had bought Sunshine's story.

'OK, that's fine then,' my father-in-law said, speaking for the first time. 'Yes, our Priya is a very helpful girl indeed,' he said, turning to Sunshine and smiling a rare smile. 'Now, *beti*,' he said, looking back at me, 'if your job is done, please go and change.'

As they left, Malini asked if I got to keep any of the clothes 'after that trashy actress is done wearing 'em'. Once they were safely in the elevator, I turned to Sunshine, humiliated.

'Don't worry about it,' she said. 'Shanisse filled me

in on your domestic situation. Wow. The drama! Great movie material!'

I was thankful to Shanisse, although my friendship with her had cooled. Unlike the days when I worked behind the reception desk, when she would tell me what she was working on, who she was meeting, what premiere she had just attended, and delighted me with stories about the outrageousness of Lynette Dove's life, she now barely said anything. Even though we chatted a little in the ladies' room or when we passed one another in the corridors, there were no more lunches together or grabbed cups of coffee in the cafeteria.

In her mind, once I had stopped being the receptionist and became her equal, I had also stopped being her friend.

Lynette, I knew, had never liked me, and mostly looked at me like a pimple that refused to go away.

'What, another one of those insipid little features?' I once overheard her saying to Crispin. 'Who wants to read about what the stars *feel*? Who does that Priya think she is? Frigging Oprah?'

Each time I heard one of those comments, or was rebuffed by Shanisse, or was criticized by Crispin, or was kept waiting by yet another movie star, or fielded another call from Avery – who still hadn't given up – I picked up the tiny gold pendant of Durga, placed it to my forehead, and then kissed it, as if doing so would protect me from the world I was now in.

A world that, especially after the impromptu visit from

my in-laws, I profoundly wished I could tell somebody about.

As far as confidantes go, Ria would have been an obvious choice. To call sister number three 'feisty', would be an understatement in the league of 'yes, J.Lo is a *tad* high maintenance'. But trustworthy Ria was. If she said she would keep something a secret, not even bribery, begging or jugs of alcohol would get it out of her.

But Ria, I knew, would also be outraged if she knew what I had been reduced to; that a happy and honest girl like me, from a decent and respectable Delhi family, was now mimicking the life of an adulteress, lying and sneaking around.

Ria would never have put up with any of that. At university in Delhi, she majored in women's studies. She wrote her thesis on *sati* – the practice of burning widows on the funeral pyres of their husbands, the thinking being that a woman without a man was worthless. She occasionally volunteered at a halfway house for battered wives and abused daughters-in-law in one of the dingiest parts of Delhi – which my father had agreed to because it was 'charity and therefore not a real job' – and read Gloria Steinem and Susan Sontag. She believed in women's rights and 'freeing them from the shackles of India's anachronistic patriarchal system', which, when she said that to Malini during my wedding, made my sister-in-law say: 'Huh?' She was outspoken, hardly ever wore anything but black trousers and a long white shirt, didn't know how to properly drape a sari *or* finish peeling an apple before it turned brown, and was therefore not even a candidate for wifehood. As Kaki said, shaking her head, it would be 'too much work for anyone to marry Ria'.

But of all my sisters, she was probably the one I could confide in. Radha, a decade on from losing Nishant, was still immersed in grief, a feeling that seemed to have deepened after I had got married. Roma, on the other hand, was so much in love with the *idea* of one day becoming a wife that it would break her heart to know that I had to lie to my husband in order to have a shot at happiness; Barbara Cartland, she would say to me, had *never* written anything like that. My mother would instantly fly over and rescue me, but then I would become just another disenfranchised Indian girl, and I figured that if I was going to be that, I was better off in Los Angeles than in Delhi.

There were times when I thought perhaps I could tell Sanjay everything – the job, the clothes, the accomplishments, everything. But then I would see how he would side with his mother on even the most petty domestic details, and it occurred to me that I still wasn't confident enough in my husband's love for me to take that kind of a chance. Fundamentally, I didn't believe that, when push came to shove, he wouldn't shove me out of the house.

23

I had read in last month's issue of *Glamour* that the way to foster a sense of closeness with someone was to lure them slowly into your life, to 'make them an integral part of the various aspects of your everyday existence', which I thought was a very fancy way of saying 'take them out'.

So that's why I was going to ask Sanjay to escort me to a premiere.

'It's the new Niles Ardent film,' James had said to me. 'It's won at Cannes, lots of Oscar buzz. Surely you've heard of it?'

Like everyone else in my family – or in India, for that matter – if a movie didn't star Sylvester Stallone, I hadn't a clue. My nation's biggest stars, Sanjay Dutt and Salman Khan, lifted weights and sprinted on treadmills to build their bodies like Sly, or at least that is what I had read in *Vivacious!* Where I came from, we liked movies like *Rambo*, long epics with broken bones and crushed hearts.

But Niles Ardent was one of those rising stars who didn't really look like one. He was far too thin, far too pale, with long nostrils and droopy eyes that made him look like a cartoon character. He wasn't like Brad Pitt, a real leading man, pictures of whom covered the walls of the bedrooms of friends of mine in Delhi, and might have even done so in my house if my father had allowed it.

'Go along and see what the movie is like, and then perhaps we'll send you off to chat with him,' James had said.

When I called Sanjay to tell him that we were going to a premiere, he was so excited that he almost forgot to remind me that I'd still need to make dinner.

'Afterwards, we can go to California Pizza Kitchen or something,' he said. 'But Mummy, Papa and Malini have to eat, so will you have time to make food for them first? Will we be home late?'

As far as he knew, I had been given two passes through someone in my office who couldn't make it. It was, I told him, a 'perk', a little way for one of my superiors to thank me for my diligent phone-answering work.

The name of the movie, *Last Best Hope*, flashed brightly atop the Westwood theatre. Outside, passers-by had stopped to see what was going on, while paparazzi jostled one another to click away as dozens of famous people stepped out of limos. Sanjay stood next to me, his mouth slightly open, one finger lightly touching a velvet rope, staring at the fracas in front of him.

'Look, Priya, there's even a red carpet,' he said, nudging me. I looked down, and noticed that it was not quite red – more like a dirty burgundy, soiled from years of use. Sanjay and I stood on the edge of it, me wearing a turquoise silk sari, he in a jacket and tie. I was about to put one foot on the length of dark red, holding my husband's hand, both of us treading delicately as if we were about to step into the holy water of the River Ganges.

'Excuse me, miss, where are you going?' a security man, brandishing two walkie-talkies, and badges up and down his sleeve, asked me.

'Oh, inside. To the premiere. The movie,' I said.

'This here red carpet is for VIPs only. Who are you?' He looked at the ticket I was holding up, the words *Hollywood Insider* neatly typed across it.

'Non-VIPs get in over there,' he said, directing me to a side entrance. 'Please, get out of the way. The stars are arriving.'

We were given coupons for complimentary popcorn and sodas, which I was too embarrassed to use, thinking that people dressed nicely shouldn't be lining up for free refreshments.

'Don't be silly, Priya,' Sanjay said, snatching the coupons out of my hand. 'Give, I'll go do it. You find seats.'

Most of the rows inside were cordoned off with sticky yellow crime scene-style tape, marked 'Reserved'. Else-where, people had draped coats, bags and shawls over spare seats, evidently saving them for others. Ushers rushed up and down the aisles, too busy to stop.

'Excuse me, is anyone sitting here?' I asked a man with a mouthful of popcorn, who had two empty seats next to him.

'Saved,' he said. 'Sorry.'

Sanjay finally appeared carrying a slim cardboard box filled with cups of Cola the size of a bathtub, and looked irritated that I was still standing.

'Quickly, Priya, otherwise all the seats will be taken. What are you doing? You are with a magazine, you can sit anywhere no? Come.' He tore away part of the 'Reserved' tape and made his way down the aisle, pulling me down onto a seat next to him in the centre.

Behind us, two girls were dissecting the famous and less-famous women that were being escorted down the aisle.

'Look, there's Pasha Rodriguez.' One girl pointed to a gorgeous Spanish actress who was dating one of Hollywood's biggest stars. 'She's *much* prettier in person. But look, is that a panty-line? What was she thinking?' A gleeful Niles strolled by, surrounded by an entourage, casting a proud gaze across the room like he was a head of state. Shortly behind him was Maia Mourtos, escorted by a handsome dark-haired man, looking more beautiful than ever. People were rushing up to say hello to her, but I stayed firmly in my seat.

A couple sat down to next to us, the woman complimenting me on my 'costume'.

'Beautiful colour,' she said. 'Is that one of those Middle-Eastern outfits?'

'Indian,' I said.

'Whatever,' she replied.

Within the first ten minutes of the movie starting, Sanjay asked me three times what it was about.

'Just watch it,' I whispered to him. 'It's meant to be *really* good. Just because nobody has shot anyone yet doesn't mean you should get bored.'

'Why can't you get invited to something that has Jean Claude Van Damme in it?' he asked.

Five minutes later, I glanced over at him to discover he was asleep, his head drooping, a smidgen of a snore so small that only I could hear it, and only if I pressed my ear right against his face. I let him sleep, while I struggled to keep my own eyes open. I should have read the press notes before getting here because, like my husband, I was baffled as to the plot. In my estimation, a good movie involved melodrama, humour, romance and a song or two, the elements needed to satisfy the soul through the silver screen. Here, my own last best hope was making it through the next 149 minutes without dozing off, as I tried to make sense of the Swedish setting, a symbolic feather, a very sad Niles Ardent, his one-legged mother and a fat black cat.

As soon as the last scene ended – something about a thumb being chopped off, with Niles Ardent screaming horrifically into the camera – applause rang out through the auditorium, making me feel that Sanjay and I were the only two people there not to have understood what we had just seen. As we stood up and flicked the popcorn remnants off our clothes, I noticed people around us sniggering, rolling their eyes, or just waking up. The geographically-challenged woman next to me even used the word 'crap'. But as Niles Ardent made his way back up the aisle towards the exit, they gathered around him, kissing and hugging and congratulating.

'Magnificent work!' said one. 'What thought-provoking stuff!'

I held tightly on to Sanjay's hand so as not to lose him in the crowd, and wasn't able to relax until we had made it to the foyer. Just as we were walking towards the exit, I heard a voice call my name.

'Hi, Priya, how lovely to see you again!' Maia Mourtos said gaily, her dark eyes surprisingly bright given the depressing fare they had just witnessed.

Sanjay turned round and stared at us.

'Oh, hi, Ms Mourtos. This is my husband, Sanjay,' I said, praying that she would just go away.

'Wonderful to meet you,' she said to Sanjay, before turning her stunning face back to me.

'I so enjoyed tea the other day,' she said. 'I'm hosting a – '

She was interrupted by Niles grabbing her from behind and kissing her fondly on her cheek. As she turned round and was subsumed into the girth of his group, I took Sanjay's hand and we quickly sprinted off.

'You know *her*?' he asked, eyes wide open, as star-struck as Malini might have been had she been here. 'How do you know *her*? And what was that thing about tea?'

'Oh, nothing,' I said, walking quickly to our car. 'Somebody at the office kept her waiting and I ran out and made her *chai*. That's it,' I said, hoping the interrogation would stop right there. 'Come on, let's hurry,' I added. 'We might have to wait for a table.'

24

Cosmopolitan also had other sage advice for young couples: take time to be alone. Spend intimate moments together. Indulge in romantic getaways.

As Sanjay and I sat silently in the car on our way home, I thought that perhaps that was what our marriage needed – that after more than six months together, it was time for a relationship jolt, something to wake us up. We needed to wrap ourselves in fluffy white bathrobes and sit on a terrace somewhere watching the sunset, drinking frosted pineapple juice.

Realistically, though, I knew that probably wouldn't ever happen. Sanjay, as I had discovered in our time together, was adamantly against leaving the side of his parents, even for a weekend. After two heart attacks and that nasty bathtub fall, his father had become Sanjay's biggest concern. My husband was certain that the Gods were so much against him that something would happen to his father the second Sanjay turned his back to cater to his own needs. That was why Sanjay worked with him, and that was why we all lived together.

'I am the only son,' he said to me once. 'They can't do without me. God forbid, we are out of the house and Papa falls again, or his heart stops, or he has a stroke, what will happen? How will I ever forgive myself?

The downside of this extreme filial piety, however, was that Sanjay and I would probably never really learn to know one another.

We had honeymooned in Naini Tal, at the foot of the Himalayas. Our first night there, as Sanjay paid the driver, I stood in the centre of a dusty-floored open-air courtyard, lined by stores selling disposable cameras and bulky candles in the shapes of Hindu deities. From somewhere in the distance, I heard a song from an old Hindi film, a movie that I knew my parents had gone to see together as newlyweds. The lyrics were about breathtaking beauty hidden beneath a gilt-embroidered veil, and about a love so strong that the brilliance of a new moon paled in comparison. I closed my eyes and listened, and felt for a second as my mother must have on her own honeymoon, over thirty years ago, and I longed to be her child again.

Over the next few days, it became evident to me that Sanjay and I were not that different from all the other honeymooning couples brought together by equally

216

practical alliances. The brides were defined by their newly hennaed hands, shining gold jewellery and stiff clothes, the grooms by their tentativeness at affection. Souvenir-selling photographers crowded around us at every sightseeing stop-off point, eager to make their thirty rupees for a shot. At certain times, Sanjay relented and let them snap away with their old-style Polaroids, and posed for them with his arm slung over my shoulder. Often, he made bunny ears over my head with his fingers, which caused me to giggle.

But I saw that his mind was elsewhere. Twice a day, he called his parents in Delhi, and forced me to take the phone to greet them also.

'We've just seen them,' I would reason with him. 'We'll be back with them again in a few weeks. We're on our honeymoon.'

But he didn't listen.

'Anything can happen any time; we need to be in constant touch,' he said, rummaging through his bag for rupees to pay for yet another call. 'They expect it.'

On our last night, Sanjay felt feverish, so took to our bed. I remained in one corner of our hotel room, watching television. My mother-in-law called to berate me about letting her son fall ill.

'He's your responsibility!' she shrieked. 'What are you doing to my *beta*?'

Her admonishments lingered in my ears as the entire city of Naini Tal then fell prey to a blackout. I sat alone in the dark, while my husband snored and wheezed beside me. I had thought a honeymoon could be many things, but I had never imagined that it could be this.

Before Sanjay and I had left for our new life in America, I had asked him to take me to Agra, one last time. It was just three hours from my family's home in Delhi, but I had rarely visited. There it was, one of the most astoundingly beautiful pieces of architecture in the world virtually in my backyard, and I was lucky if I saw it every few years. His mother had wanted to come too, but had developed a rash on her stomach right after the wedding, and was too busy scratching it to pack. For this, I was grateful.

I had hoped that in seeing the Taj Mahal together, Sanjay and I might be eternally spellbound by romance. This was, after all, the Mecca for honeymooners, a monument to the grandest love of all time. I had hoped that perhaps some of that magic might dislodge from the vast, rambling chunks of marble, and attach itself to us, binding us together for ever.

As we stood outside the rusting metal gates, their spokes embedded in crumbling brick walls, I could only think that it might be years before I ever saw the Taj Mahal again.

Some of my father's overseas visitors had been mesmerized not just by the Mahal, but by the lore behind it.

'Oh my Gawd, that is *so* romantic!' a curly-haired

American woman had gushed, whose husband was selling my father pylons. 'Imagine that, this big old palace that that guy built 'cos his wife died. Imagine having a guy do that!'

She, like so many other people I had met, naturally assumed that there must be something mystical about being so close to Agra, that perhaps there was something in the soil and water that infiltrated the senses and crept into the blood, and turned everyone into hopeless romantics with bountiful resources.

So I wanted to take it all in, as if staring at it long enough would allow me to transport the Taj with me. Over the years, I had seen its many faces: its glorious curves and swirling arches glinting in the hot summer sun, or forlorn beneath the monsoon rains. Somehow, like a dear friend who seldom came to visit, I still knew it intimately.

Coming here seemed a fitting way to say goodbye to my old life. I bowed my head and said a prayer for the Shah Jahan and his eternally beloved Mumtaz, as I always did, let Sanjay take my hand, and walked off with him quietly, suddenly feeling close to him. He kissed me on my forehead, wiped away a tear that was dribbling down my warm cheek, and smiled his handsome smile.

It was at that instant, I believed, that love began.

But now, six months later, I could feel it ebbing away into the crowded Los Angeles night.

25

It was barely dawn when Malini woke me up, knocking on our bedroom door before creaking it open. In the still-dark room, I made out her slim silhouette framed against the door.

'Your phone, *bhabi*,' she whispered. 'It's your mummy.'

Fear fluttered around my heart. It wasn't Sunday, and it was the wrong time of day. The only reason my mother would be calling me this early was because there was bad news. Last week, my father had had what my mother described as a 'sinister pain' in his chest that had eventually subsided. But I could only assume the worst. In a pique of paranoia, no doubt a function of maturing into a married woman, I said a quick and urgent prayer that my father was OK.

'Mamma?' I said quietly into the phone. 'Why are you calling? What has happened?'

'Darling, did I wake you?' my mother asked, sounding excited, while I exhaled. If it *was* bad news, she wouldn't take the time to enquire about whether I'd been asleep or not.

'You know, darling, I can *never* figure out the time difference, it's all totally a mystery to me. But I was rather excited to tell you something. Do you remember Ganga, Daddy's cousin's wife's sister from Madras? They were at your wedding?'

'No, Ma, I don't know who you are talking about,' I said, wanting to get back into bed again.

'Well darling, it's quite the scandal, but her daughter Karishma *eee-loped*! With an American! She was doing her Master's at Berkeley, and met someone and they ran off together! I think after her family recovered, they invited Karishma and her new husband – Steve-Beev-something-something – to India to meet everyone. Anyway, darling, Ganga tells me that they are now settled in Los Angeles. Really, you *must* call her. Become friends. It will be so nice for you to know someone from home, hah?

'And aside from all that, darling, how are you?' she asked. 'All is well, I hope? And your in-laws? They are treating you well, no?' she queried. 'You know, your daddy and I still are not happy that you are working, darling. We thought we had married you off to people of means, that you could become a lady of leisure, like that sister-in-law of yours.'

'Everyone is treating me well, Mummy. Especially Sanjay. Please don't worry about me. I'm married now. I can look after myself. Just think about the other girls.'

'I am, darling. And I pray that they will eventually find the same happiness as you.'

I didn't have to call Karishma. Apparently her mother had phoned her and told her all about me. She called at home a few evenings later. As soon as I heard her voice, I knew I would like her.

'Are you enjoying it here?' she asked politely, her accent diluted after a few years in America, but still happily sing-song. As my in-laws listened in, I told her about my receptionist job, and she remarked how much she liked the *Hollywood Insider* and how lucky I was to be working there. She was a business consultant, which sounded like a very important job, although I had no idea what it actually meant. Her husband, Steve, whom she met while at Berkeley, was a psychotherapist.

'He specializes in marriage counselling,' she said proudly. 'He's better than Dr Phil. Obviously that makes him a great husband as well,' she continued. 'So, listen, why don't we meet for a drink? The after-work scene by the pool at the Avalon is great,' she said.

'I think maybe daytime is better for me,' I replied.

Karishma didn't work far from me, so we set up a lunch date later in the week. That morning, I agonized for forty minutes about my wardrobe, more than I did when I interviewed famous people or went on movie junkets, as they didn't care and never noticed anyway.

But Karishma was one of those smart, liberated Indian

women, the kind who married for love and went bicycle-riding with their husband at weekends and talked openly about everything and didn't have to steam carrots every night for a gastrically challenged father-in-law. She was Indian, but not. She was the kind of woman who, no matter how long I stayed in this country and how pretty my clothes were, I would never become. She was free, and I never would be.

We had arranged to meet at the Italian restaurant with the yellow awning. I watched her through the big glass window, pushing a button on her key-chain to activate the alarm on her car, and pulling her sunglasses off her face. Although she was in a pale beige trouser suit, a pretty blue shawl draped around her shoulders, she reminded me of an athlete – tall, lean, moving with confidence. She smiled and waved when she saw me in the corner of the restaurant, and her short, swept-back hair barely moved as she glided towards me.

'I knew it was you,' she said, reaching out her hand. 'My mother showed me pictures of your wedding. Beautiful.'

'Thank you,' I said, half-standing up and motioning her to sit in the chair opposite me. 'I've ordered some lemonade. Would you like the same?'

Karishma was a few years older than me, far more educated, and loved to talk. Even before our drinks were served, she told me how she met Steve (her Frisbee almost smacked him in the stomach), where they married (on a boat moored off a beach in Maui, just her and him

224

and a minister) and how her parents reacted to the news (mother fainted, father exploded, brother took the momentous news as licence to inform everyone that he was gay). She called Steve her 'soul mate', her one-and-only.

'We lived together first,' she said, causing me to drop my bread roll. 'But I never told my parents *that*. And, of course, I agonized about marrying outside the community, but he was *so* understanding and patient, so willing to listen to me. Where are you going to find that in an Indian guy?' she said, spearing her fork into some frisée lettuce.

'Oh, sorry, I don't mean to imply that *your* husband isn't understanding and patient,' she continued. 'I'm sure he's lovely.' She nodded, not convincingly. 'But I had never met anyone like that, and believe me, I looked. I mean, where was I going to find an Indian boy that wasn't a mamma's boy? Oh, sorry, I didn't mean for you to feel that your husband is like that, but – '

'It's OK,' I said, interrupting her. 'You don't have to keep apologizing for your opinions. It's just good that you found the right person to be with.'

Karishma laughed easily and often, her dark eyes sparkling beneath her fringe. As she lifted a coffee cup to her lips, I noticed her heart-shaped diamond engagement ring, and complimented her on it.

'Stunning, isn't it?' she said, gazing at her hand and smiling proudly. 'Steve searched high and low for something that he felt would reflect his feelings for me.'

225

I looked down at my ring finger, on which sat the shiny round diamond that Sanjay had given me the day of our engagement. He hadn't even seen it until he had slipped it onto my finger; the stone, I found out later, had been part of a necklace owned by my mother-in-law, which had been disassembled, the diamond removed, and affixed into a platinum band for an engagement ring. My mother-in-law had taken care of all the details, while my father-in-law had paid for it. Sanjay had nothing to do with it. Fearing that the ring was broadcasting its impersonal and solely symbolic status, I placed both my hands under my thighs, and firmly sat on them.

'Not that it's been easy, marrying an outsider,' she said. 'Our first few days in Madras, we went to a tiny place for lunch – you know, the hole-in-the-wall type that has the best *dosas* in town. You know what Steve asked the waiter? If they had avocados! I said to him, "Darling, where do you think you are, the Santa Monica Farmers' Market?" And people looked at us funny, like I had done something absolutely treacherous, that I couldn't have done better. Somebody told me a long time ago that it's a profound shame for an Indian girl to marry outside, as if in so doing we are lost for ever,' she said, her eyes suddenly looking forlorn. 'I don't feel lost, but I can see their point.

'Anyway, Priya,' she said, gathering her thoughts and calling for the bill, 'I've been in America for a few years now. I know what it's like to be new here. So if you need anything, just someone to talk to even, please call me, OK? Think of me as your older sister.'

'I already have three,' I said. 'But thank you very much.'

26

The dream rarely changed.

I was in a pink polyester nightgown, holding a black suitcase, walking down the long dark street in the rain. I got to the front door of my house in Delhi, trees with fleshy mangoes bowing to greet me, brass wind chimes singing in the soaked breeze. Drenched, I stood there, and slowly raised my finger to ring the doorbell. Kaki opened the door, looked down at the suitcase and then into my despairing eyes, clutched at her heart, and fell to the floor.

This is the reason, as married Hindu women, that we can never go back.

Work became my sanctuary. At the office, people talked about not being able to wait to go home, to reuniting with their spouses and children and reality shows and microwaved dinners.

But I couldn't wait to come to work, escaping the tiled kitchen with its heady spicy smells that had infiltrated every corner of the house.

The office, even with its attendant politics and rumour-mongering and deadlines, became my safe house.

Instead of the one-on-one interviews that I was often sent on, I preferred going on movie junkets, which Crispin would dispatch me to when nobody else was either interested or available. Here I could be a silent part of a 'round table' of journalists interviewing the 'talent'. Before the star arrived, I would listen quietly to the others chat, saying things like: 'I've been waiting for Hugh Grant to get back to more serious fare'. I could sit in my chair and be quiet, observing as the other reporters competed to get a question in, trying to be impressive and memorable. There was always one person at the table that everyone else called the 'question hog', because he would latch on to a movie star and not let go.

'Gina says hi,' a journalist threw out with surprising familiarity to an A-list star on my first junket, evidently wanting everyone else in the room to know that he was only separated from a famous person by just one other individual.

Sometimes, I forced myself to ask a question, and would wait until the publicist was in the room, so they would at least think that I was knowledgeable and engaged. But usually I felt that everyone else's questions were sharper than my own, based on some kernel of news they had been privy to, while the best I could do was unchallenging stuff like: 'What has been your favourite role so far?', which usually caused everyone else at the table to roll their eyes.

Crispin often talked to me about having to 'toughen you up'.

'Your writing skills are better, but you need to be less slavish about pleasing everyone,' he said. 'Learn where the line is.'

As was usually the case, I had no idea what he was talking about.

As I had hoped we would, Karishma and I became friends – regular, ongoing, let's-say-we'll-have-lunch-and-mean-it friends. She didn't want to call me at work, fearing that it would interfere with my other supposed phone-answering duties, so we shot emails to one another back and forth. In so doing, I developed a closeness to her that I felt I was beginning to lose with my sisters, the fact that they were thousands of miles away not helping any. Karishma was, to me, a girl who understood – a girl who had at one time kept secrets from her family, yet who had eventually come to clarify her connection not just to the country she came from, but the one she had moved to.

'I have something to tell you,' I said to Karishma one day, as we sat on a park bench and munched on sandwiches.

'You're pregnant! I knew it!' she said, putting her hand on my tummy.

'No, that's not it,' I replied. 'It's something else, something I can't tell anyone.'

'What is it?' she asked, her face suddenly serious, her turkey roll laying in its Cellophane wrap atop her lap.

'I'm actually not a receptionist. I am a journalist.' I realized that I had never uttered those words before. 'I write for the *Hollywood Insider*. My in-laws would throw me out of the house if they found out. They wanted me to have a simple job, so they think I'm a receptionist. Everyone thinks that. Except, now, for you.'

Karishma listened as I told her how I had come to be doing this. When I was finished, she leaned over and put her arms around my neck and hugged me close to her, like my mother had done on my wedding night.

'I'm so sorry you have to go through all this,' she said. I felt a lump develop in my throat, and my eyes tear up. Few things are sadder than empathy.

'Why don't you come over and meet Steve some time? Maybe he can help you sort this out in your head. Really, he's just so wonderful to talk to.'

'Pretentious piffle, wasn't it?' James said about the Niles Ardent movie, when I ran into him in the elevator.

'I didn't really understand it,' I replied. 'When we got home, my sister-in-law asked my husband what he thought, and he told her to take a pillow.'

'That bad, eh?' he grinned broadly. 'Well then, you'll love this: we've set up for you to interview Ardent tomorrow. I hear his newfound fame has gone to his head a bit, so you'll have to use all your charm to get him to say anything.'

'I'd really rather not do it,' I said, stepping out on my floor. 'I don't care for him, or the movie, or for anything he's done before. I'm not interested in him.'

'Priya, my dear, this is celebrity journalism. What you're interested in is completely irrelevant.'

I had never been late to an interview before. But that morning, I had a very good reason. I had gone to meet Karishma, and she had brought along Steve. They were at the Coffee Bean before me, and had taken up a corner table, their drinks already ordered. Despite all Karishma's descriptions of them being a God-created couple, perfect in every way, they didn't really look like they belonged together. She was all dark-haired excitability, clad in high heels and urbane clothes, he was red-topped and freckled, a hooded sweatshirt hanging off his skinny frame, sandals on long feet. But when they stood to greet me, his smile was warm and beckoning. He hugged me hello as I clenched my body in discomfort, realizing that no man had held me that close except Sanjay.

'I've heard so much about you from Kar,' he said, fondling his wife's fingers. 'I hope you don't mind, but she filled me in on your situation. Fascinating.'

'It's good for me to have her to talk to,' I said. 'I have nobody else.'

Over warm blueberry muffins and cappuccino, Steve analysed me. I had heard something about this thing called therapy, which I understood from television that lots of people in America did, as a hobby almost. This, however, was not that. There was no couch for me to recline on, no box of Kleenex to resort to. As lone people around us typed away on laptop computers and chatted endlessly on their mobiles, Steve and I talked about my life, his hand entwined with that of his wife the whole time.

'You look so happy,' I said, addressing them both, 'even though you are different from one another.'

'Yes, she is my precious one,' Steve said, gently lifting up Karishma's hand and kissing it. 'I can't imagine what my life would be like without her. She teaches me something everyday.'

I felt stirrings of what I recognized as envy rising from somewhere in my belly. Sanjay had never spoken either to me, or of me, with such tenderness – and he would certainly never show me that degree of affection in public. Karishma was almost American now, but she knew that, where we came from, couples don't let their lips touch together in public, even on their wedding day.

'You know that I'm not here to judge you, right?' Steve said, looking at me earnestly. 'Your choices are your own. But dishonesty is never a good idea, under any circumstances. It's always easy to blame other people, or the circumstances you are in. But more often than not the only way out is to confront the things you

234

fear the most – in this case, the loss of your husband's love. Confront it, and challenge yourself to deal with whatever happens as a consequence.'

The tears started again, but I had to stop them. Niles Ardent was waiting for me.

If there is one thing I had learned having been an entertainment reporter for all these months, it was that actors *never* want to hear the truth about their performances, or the quality of the movie they were just in. Even if they beseech you to tell them – truly, honestly, what did you think? – heaven help you if you seem less than enthused.

Somehow, I thought Niles Ardent would be different. He was an intellectual, profoundly cultured, allegedly averse to the whole 'Hollywood scene'. He read Nietzsche and performed on the London stage in his spare time. He was a *serious* actor.

I could tell as much when he stood up to greet me in his suite at the Chateau Marmont hotel, tiny spectacles poised to slip down his steep nose. He spoke in an indeterminate accent, as if he wasn't quite sure if he should be British (which he was by birth) or American (which is what Hollywood wanted him to be). He was wearing cashmere and drinking chamomile tea. The only things missing were a pipe, and a basset hound by his side.

I glanced down my list of prepared questions, which James had helped me formulate. After all this time, I was still nervous, still fearful of betraying my ignorance. It always haunted me that other journalists could rattle off names of decades-old films and obscure directors, as if they lived for the movies. I still had no idea what the difference was between a *film noir* and a spaghetti western. To me, if it didn't star Meg Ryan and Tom Hanks and involve cupfuls of sweetness, I knew nothing about it.

Niles had a welcoming face, young but creased with kindness. It was obvious that he was a fairly relaxed and happy chap, so I didn't understand why he had chosen to make so morose a film.

'So, Mr Ardent, what drew you to this role?' I asked, pushing the 'Record' button on my tape recorder. 'Why did you say yes to it, or why, conversely do you feel it came to you?'

'Well, that's pretty obvious, isn't it?' he said, one thinly sliced eyebrow arching up. 'What a magnificent role! Full of potential! Couldn't you tell? Didn't you just love it?'

I was quiet, my eyes on the beige folder on my lap.

'Well, didn't you?' he asked. 'Everyone is raving.'

'Well, I . . . how to put this? I didn't *understand* it, sir. It baffled me. My husband too.'

The actor sat back in his chair, smugness spreading across his face.

'Let me guess,' he said. 'Probably the most mentally challenging thing you've seen recently was something from Eddie Murphy, right? Can't take anything a bit more layered? Does it all have to be mindless fluff? Have you fallen victim to big-studio crap as well?' His words were sharp, his stare now bitter. I wanted to switch off my tape recorder, and leave.

'No, sir, nothing like that. I also like serious movies. Dramas and all. But maybe this movie, maybe it's just too complex for me. I apologize for not enjoying it.'

Our interview was the shortest ever – seven minutes – and then he said he had to be excused, something important had to be dealt with. As I left the hotel, the shame I felt caused me to cry. But Niles Ardent, I knew, had nothing to do with it.

I felt shamed because my marriage was dying, and I had no idea how to rescue it. But what saddened me the most was that if it hadn't been for Karishma and Steve and the example of their union, I probably would never even have known it.

27

Barely fifteen minutes into *The Hours*, Sanjay was dozing off on the couch. It was a splendidly quiet Saturday afternoon, the rest of the family out, just Sanjay and I at home.

I had been keen to see the movie, and while Sanjay's first pick was the Austin Powers sequel, he gave in to my request. But now, after the opening credits rolled, he was already asleep. I poked him in the arm.

'What?' he said, rubbing his elbow. 'What did you wake me up for? You can watch this. I'm taking a nap.'

'It's meant to be a beautiful and poetic movie,' I said. 'Can't you at least try and stay awake for it?'

'I just don't get it,' he said. 'What are all these chicks whining about? It's not like they are poor or sick or anything. Jeez.'

I paused the film, and turned to look at him.

'Sanjay, do you not think it's possible for a woman to have everything yet still be unhappy?'

'Oh, honey, please. It's a Saturday. Let's not get into

239

a big discussion about the girls in this film, OK?'

'I'm not just talking about the movie,' I said quietly, now turning the DVD player off. 'I'm talking about women generally. Actually, I'm talking about me.'

Sanjay sat upright, his boyish face blank. He had probably heard from his few American friends about women wanting to have these 'talks'. But I could tell by the nondescript expression in his eyes that he evidently believed Indian men didn't need to have these conversations with their equally Indian wives.

'Priya, why so serious?' he said, putting his arm round me and pulling me close. 'It's a nice lovely Saturday. Hey, let's go for mini-golf or something,' he said, starting to rise from the sofa.

'You know, in almost one year of marriage, you have never told me that you love me,' I said, my words stopping him. 'I've been waiting to hear those words. Nobody has ever said them to me.' I was crying now. 'I was hoping you would be the first.'

'Of *course* I do,' he said, stopping and turning round to look at me again. 'You know, in our family, we don't say these things. That's just how we are. It's not like all these Americans, where everything has to be said all the time.' He forced a laugh. 'Come on, let's go do something fun.'

Vivacious! once said that the key to a lasting and fulfilling marriage is to remember the happy moments, to focus on the tiny kindnesses that make the union at least bearable, if not delightful. Like how I didn't really mind it when I cut my finger, because I loved the way Sanjay placed a Band-Aid on it, peeling off the adhesive and delicately setting in place the slim flesh-coloured tape. Or when he would massage my shoulders for a few moments after I had spent three hours stirring mango and condensed milk for his favourite dessert. Those were the things that, in the face of mounting loneliness, made me want to stay close. And really, it wasn't as if I had any other place to go.

'Sanjay, this is Steve and Karishma. This is my husband, Sanjay.'

The four of us were standing in a basement car park, having run into one another outside Target on a Sunday evening. Steve and Karishma were wheeling a red cart filled with what they call 'home accents' in this country: chenille cushions, thick blankets to drape over a couch, and, peeking out of a bag, a martini pitcher with glasses. I imagined them going home with their new purchases, spreading them out and laying them down and trying them on, and then fixing a dinner of *fajitas* and margaritas and watching something from Blockbuster, canoodling over popcorn.

Sanjay and I were going in to look for electric heaters – my father-in-law said that our gas bill was too high and we were forbidden from using the central heating in the house – and a new toilet bowl brush. After that, we were to go to the Asian market on Victory and Sepulveda to buy beansprouts and tofu, because Malini had a craving for Chinese and nobody had thought of ordering in. I would be stir-frying for the rest of the night.

'So *great* to meet you!' Steve said, grabbing Sanjay by his hand and then pulling in to him for a hug. 'Heard so much about you from Priya.'

'What a coincidence, running into you here!' Karishma said brightly. 'Love this store. Hey, listen, maybe when you're done with your shopping we can meet up later, grab a bite? There's a new *tapas* bar I've been wanting to try out,' she said.

'Sorry, can't,' Sanjay replied. 'We have to have dinner with my parents. We're cooking.'

'Actually, *I'm* cooking,' I corrected him. 'Thanks for the invitation though. Another time?'

'So *that's* your new friend,' Sanjay said later, as we wheeled our cart down the endless aisles. 'Nice-looking girl. What, she couldn't find an Indian guy to marry?'

'Sanjay! What a terrible thing to say! They love each other!' I said, now irate at my husband's shallowness. 'What, you think Steve is some kind of default husband?'

'I just don't want you getting too close to them,' he said, reading the instructions on the back of a box. 'They don't look to be our type of people.'

The impromptu meeting that night was especially awkward because Steve and I had already begun our 'sessions'. He did tell me that most of his marriage counselling clients came as a couple, that it almost defeated the purpose of the exercise if there was just one despairing soul in the room with him. But he understood it when I told him that to Sanjay, there was nothing wrong with us. Our marriage was perfection itself, our lives a godsend. Therapy, he had told me when I casually mentioned it one day in some random context, was for 'serial killers and people with alcoholic fathers, and that's usually the same thing.'

I don't know what Sanjay would have done had he known that, once a week, on a Monday lunchtime, I drove over to Steve and Karishma's Santa Monica home, where, on a black couch covered with embroidered yellow cushions in a guesthouse in the back was where he helped resurrect dilapidated spirits.

'Who are you trying to please?' he asked me, pushing a Lucite box that had been filled with snow-white Kleenex towards me. 'What are you most afraid of?'

It took three weeks before I could even answer his questions. Until then, during my hour – which was being given to me at the discounted 'friend's' fee of $50 instead of the usual $125 – I evaded Steve's questions and talked generally and almost positively about my marriage and my life.

'Do you think maybe you drew Sanjay into your life to make up for having a distant and emotionally detached father?' he asked, as I blinked in confusion. 'Perhaps you are hoping that Sanjay will give you the love you never had from daddy.'

'My daddy loves me,' I said, tearing again. 'And I love

243

Sanjay. Don't you think he's good-looking? I could imagine that he could have had any girl for a wife, and he chose me. And it's a nice house we live in. He's a good provider. And don't you think he's handsome?' I asked again.

'What I think is not the issue,' Steve replied. 'What is, is how you feel. You don't need to justify your life to me. I'm not here to judge anything. My goal is to ensure your happiness, by helping you to see things clearly. Look, there's a workshop I think you might benefit from,' he said. 'But it's not going to work unless Sanjay goes with you. You somehow have to find a way to get him there.'

That night, I studied the glossy brochure that Steve had slipped into my bag. 'Take yourself to a new level of intimacy and connection with your partner/lover/spouse,' it read. 'Find the path to true love by eliminating old blockages.'

I knew Sanjay would never go for it. He would scoff if I even reiterated those words, and would say something predictable like: 'We don't need intimacy and connection. We're married.'

But I also knew my husband well enough to know that if there was one thing he would never turn down, it was the offer of something free. As was the habit of his parents, if he didn't have to pay for it, it wouldn't matter what it was. He would be the first one there.

'Wow, weekend vacation. Cool,' he said, lying on the bed while I packed two small duffel bags. We were leaving the next morning, and I had just spent most of dinner listening to my mother-in-law gripe about our impending forty-eight-hour absence.

'What's the special occasion that you two have to go off like that?' she frowned, squeezing together tiny mountains of *chapatti* and potatoes and flinging them into her mouth with oil-covered fingers. 'It's not your anniversary yet. Or nobody's birthday. Who will do all the work here?'

Sanjay chewed on his food in silence for a minute before speaking.

'It's free, Mumma,' he said. 'We don't have to pay anything – even food and everything is included, yes, Priya? And maybe there'll be a raffle or something. Maybe we can win a new stereo. What harm is there to go? Priya's office has given it to her because she does such good work there. Last time, it was the premiere. This time, a weekend retreat for two. I'm sure everything will be fine with daddy for a couple of days.'

'You should have asked them for three more places,' my father-in-law said. 'We could all have come with you.'

Later, as I gathered a few things for the weekend, Sanjay asked me if there was a leaflet that he could look at.

'Is it like Club Med? Are we going to the beach? Can I play volleyball?' he asked.

'It's a surprise,' I said to him, anxiety swirling in my stomach. 'I don't know about sporting facilities, but you'll love it. I promise.' I knew I shouldn't be misleading him, but I didn't even consider the consequences. I just had to get him there.

The traffic out of the city was so bad that we didn't make it to the venue until after nine in the evening. Sanjay had been driving but, even so, I was convinced that we had taken the wrong turn. We pulled up a dirt road outside what looked like an old farmhouse, surrounded by a wire fence.

'What the hell is this?' Sanjay asked. 'Are you sure you got the address correct?

As I peered into my Filofax, a man walked through the door and, smiling, approached our car.

'You're the last two arrivals,' he said, bending down so his white bushy beard filled the car window. 'I'll open the gate for you. Keep going straight and you'll find a place to park. The rest of the group is waiting for you.'

'What the hell is this?' Sanjay repeated, as we slowly trundled along again. 'Where's the beach?'

We parked outside a large, low building. Through the windows, we saw people seated variously on plastic chairs or on the floor, listening to a couple standing on a podium in front. Leaving our things in the car, I opened the door, Sanjay following closely behind me, whispering to me to get back in the car so we could go home. I turned to face him, stared him straight in the eyes and said: 'We're here. We're staying.'

Everyone turned as we walked in. There must have

been fifty people in the room, all ages and colours, although a quick visual check confirmed that Sanjay and I were the only Indians here. I was relieved.

'Welcome!' beamed the stout, squat woman who had been addressing the gathering, a bespectacled young man by her side. 'You must be . . .' she looked down at a clipboard in her hand, tracing one finger down a list, '. . . Priya and Sanjay. Right? Am I pronouncing it correctly?'

I nodded as Sanjay stood, rock-like, next to me.

'I'm Josie,' she said, 'and this is my partner, Sam. We'll be leading the workshop. Glad you could make it, but you missed dinner. Grab a couple of chairs in the back or just sit on the floor. We're about halfway through the introduction and then we'll call it a night and start fresh tomorrow.'

Sanjay stood in the same spot while I plopped to the ground, yanking his hand downwards.

'What the hell is this?' he repeated, under his breath. 'What workshop? Where did you bring me?'

'Please, Sanjay, let's just stay a while and listen, OK?' I said.

I had originally planned to feign ignorance and surprise, to pretend that we had been sent to the wrong place but, hey, we were here now. But something about being in that room with all those seemingly sincere people, miles away in the darkness halfway up a mountain, made me feel that for now, just tonight, maybe it would be OK not to lie. I felt that if everyone else was

247

being this earnest, I owed it to them to be the same way.

Josie and Sam took turns to speak, addressing one another – and the group before them – like old friends delighted to see one another again. They spoke quietly, gently, smiling through soft and shining eyes. They looked sane, peaceful. It was the same look I had seen in Karishma and Steve, the same contentment.

'So the point of this weekend is to learn to come from a more heart-centred space,' Josie said, clasping her hands over her chest. 'We've all been there. We've all had success and material gain. Then we come home and find our emotional lives falling apart. We're dissatisfied with our relationships. We feel alone and empty. Some of us here can't find the right person to be in a relationship with. Those that are in one might be feeling adrift. It's an endless story. Over the next couple of days, through a series of exercises, we'll learn to dissolve those blockages that stand between us and our happiness. Right, Sam?' she said, turning to the slim man next to her.

'So right, Josie. And can I just add that this workshop is experiential. In order to get anything out of it, you have to put yourself into it wholly and fully. Let go of any worries about the outside world. For the next two days, it's all about you and your heart. Any questions?'

I glanced around the room and saw a smattering of raised hands, and was shocked to see, right behind me, that Sanjay's was one of them.

'Yes, to the latecomer,' Sam said, smiling, gesturing to Sanjay.

248

'Tell me, how much did my wife pay to come to this crappy place?' he said, his body stiff with anger. 'Who here brainwashed her?'

I dropped my head in embarrassment between my folded knees, while a heavy silence fell upon the room.

'You and your wife evidently have issues to work out between you,' Sam replied calmly. 'That's why you're here. And that's why we're here, to help you.'

Sanjay stood up, his legs trembling. I had never seen him so angry, and it frightened me. His usually placid and perfect face took on a greyish tinge, his eyes wide, fists clenched fiercely by his side.

'This is supposed to be Club Med,' he said. 'There is goddamn nothing wrong with me and my wife. But there is something wrong with all you crazy people. You're nuts. No culture, no community, no nothing. So you come to a stupid cult like this. If you all went home and got the blessings of your elders, maybe you wouldn't be so messed up.'

An older grey-haired woman seated a few feet from us, who had been taking in this drama with a look of intense seriousness on her face, suddenly stood up. From a multicoloured woven bag at her side, she pulled out a long cardboard tube, the kind that posters are rolled up and stored in. This one had been painted a pale pink. For the first time, I noticed that everyone in the class had the same implement next to them.

'I know you missed everything, but this here is a crucial prop for this workshop,' she said, holding the tube above her head. 'You're gonna get one too.' She pointed it towards Sanjay's chest, and I thought for a minute she was going to jab him with it, which – given how I was now feeling – would not have been such a bad idea.

'I'm going to blow into this and open your heart chakra,' she said, lifting one end of the tube to her mouth.

'Don't talk to me about chakras!' Sanjay shouted, even angrier. 'We bloody invented them before you crazy Americans came along!'

The woman let her tube drop, her eyes open in astonishment.

'Listen, you should be thanking your wife for bringing you here,' she said, looking sympathetically at me. 'You obviously come from some ossified culture – ' at this, I could see Sanjay's eyes glaze over as he tried to figure out what 'ossified' meant – 'but you're in the twenty-first century now. These days, couples *talk* about their problems. You will benefit from staying here, trust me.'

Sanjay looked down at me, bent over, and pulled me up by my elbow.

'We're leaving now,' he said, addressing Josie and Sam. 'We would like a full refund.'

'Please stay,' Josie said quietly. 'Honour your wife's wishes.'

'I'll honour nothing,' Sanjay replied, as my head spun and I felt his fingers boring into my elbow, conscious of all these strangers witnessing this, a mass of bewildered faces taking in this perverse marital drama. It shamed me – not just because I was doing the unthinkable and having a private problem aired for public consumption – but because I could tell by the knowing looks in the eyes of those around us that I had married someone I should never have married.

'Please, Sanjay,' I begged, tearful. 'Just sit. Half an hour, I promise. Then we can leave. Please. We came all the way.'

To my astonishment, Sanjay took a sharp intake of breath and lowered himself to the floor again.

'OK, but *only* for you,' he said to me, his eyes narrowed.

'Thank you,' said Sam, as Sanjay sat down again. 'Now take a deep breath, and blow out all those feelings of rage and resentment. Close your eyes, and bring to mind your special place – a forest or the lake – and visually take yourself there.'

'Funny you say that, because we should be *at* the beach,' Sanjay muttered, his eyes still open, while everyone around us laughed. I smiled. Maybe this was going to be OK after all.

Sanjay listened passively as some of the others stood up and shared their stories. After the first couple of 'shares', which I found utterly gripping – I had no idea there was this much misery in America – I could see Sanjay's mind start to wander. He began to pull the lint off his socks, as a gap-toothed woman complained about not being able to meet the right man.

'But I'm telling the universe now that I'm ready to

accept him!' she said, her voice quaking, as the others cheered and Sanjay rolled his eyes.

'She can tell the universe what she wants, but no guy is ever going to go out with her,' he whispered to me, as I jabbed him to be quiet.

Josie glanced at the clock on the wall behind us, and announced that it was time to wind down, and call it a night. Sanjay was the first one on his feet.

'Before we all rush off, let's surround ourselves in healing pink light and thank our angel guides for bringing us here,' she intoned, her eyes closed. 'We can gather for group hugs, and remember to let your hearts touch. Rest well, and we'll see you back here at nine tomorrow morning for the start of day two. It's going to be a cathartic one, so be prepared. I love you all,' she beamed.

Outside the building, people came up to Sanjay and patted him on the back.

'You're more of a man for staying,' said one long-haired fellow, who had a banjo strapped to his back. 'Peace, guy,' he said, holding up two fingers.

'We're not staying. Goodbye,' Sanjay replied, before turning to me and grabbing my arm. 'I don't know what you were thinking, Priya,' he said. 'I don't know what kind of people you work with and who talked you into something like this, and then you lie to me about it and make me waste my time and gas to drive here. I don't know what has gotten into you. I have the car keys. We're leaving.'

I stood still and pried his fingers loose.

'I think we should stay,' I said. 'We need to face things. I'm sorry I lied to you, but it was the only way to get you here.'

Sanjay stared at me, blankly.

'I'm leaving and you had better come with me,' he said.

'Then *you* go,' I said, surprised at my words. 'I'm staying here. I'll make my own way home.'

'Don't bother,' he said, staring at me one last time, and then turning and walking towards the car.

As I heard the swish-swish of his orange windcheater moving away from me, I remembered the dream: me in my nightgown, walking down our Delhi street, the look of shock and sadness in Kaki's eyes as she opened the door to her only married granddaughter, married no more.

Sanjay and I drove home in silence.

28

When a marriage starts to unravel, it's almost instantaneous. I'd seen people on the talk shows discuss the slow crumbling of sentiment, the eventual wearing away of the goodwill that is needed to sustain a union.

I'm not sure if that is always the case. I think for many couples, the end of a marriage can happen at the completion of a dinner party, or the start of a new morning, or in the middle of a silent car-ride home.

Sanjay made an excuse to his parents about a mix-up in the reservations, explaining our rather short-lived weekend vacation, and my mother-in-law made a comment about how I could never get anything right. I touched their feet, and went upstairs to bed.

The next morning, Sanjay surprised me by suggesting we go for a walk. He was quite right in thinking it would be our only way to have some privacy. Although we had barely talked since the fiasco of the night before, he looked as if he had calmed down considerably, and this relieved me no end.

Our sneakers squeaked along the quiet, cool concrete and I was aware of how ridiculous I must look in my cotton salwar kameez and Nikes on my feet. But it was a weekend, and my in-laws saw no reason for me to 'dress Western' on off-work days.

'Do you want to tell me what's going on in your head?' Sanjay asked, breaking the silence after a ten-hour stretch.

I kept my eyes down, but felt the tears coming. Until last night, before we got to the workshop, I had some hope of making my marriage happy. This morning, I didn't even have that.

'I just thought we could use some help,' I said quietly, wiping my eyes with my sleeve. 'I thought our marriage could be better. I only had good intentions, I promise.'

At that, Sanjay seemed to soften.

'Tell me what is making you unhappy,' he said. 'Tell me why you feel you have to go outside for help and advice to these stupid and useless workshops that are not for our type of people? What problems do you have? Don't you live in a good house? Don't you eat good food? Are you sick? What? What?' he asked, getting irate again.

'Sanjay, it's got nothing to do with the house or food. Marriage should be about more than that. I don't feel appreciated. We never really talk. I don't know what's happening in your life. I don't know what you're thinking about.'

'Hai, Priya, what's to know? Daddy and I are trying

to run a business, so that's what's happening in my life. And I'm thinking about paying the bills and keeping everyone comfortable and safe. That's all. What else do you expect? And what do you mean, you're not appreciated? Where is it written that I'm supposed to be grateful for a wife?'

I stopped walking, causing Sanjay to stand still as well.

'Everyone told me not to expect much from marriage,' I said quietly, remembering my Aunt Vimla. 'They said the less I expected, the happier I would become, because then every small positive thing is a treasure. But I'm sorry, I can't be that way. I want to feel happy and joyful. I want to feel close to you. I want us to have privacy. But your family interferes in everything and you always take their side. I feel like after almost a year together, we are still strangers.'

Sanjay stared at me as a cool breeze blew in from the hills in the distance, lifting up a dried leaf by his foot and making it twirl and pirouette like a lonely dancer.

'I'm sure this is something to do with your friend Karishma and her American husband,' he said, his nose twitching. 'Ever since you met them, you have become a little mad in your thinking. Unnecessarily complaining. You know, when I was in college here I had an American girlfriend. She wanted me to marry her. But like hell. I knew that she would be the kind of person who would disobey my family. That's why I came to India and found you. I didn't want a nagging-type person. But now, look, after so little time here, what have you become?'

I reached for the Kleenex that I always kept tucked away in my sleeve, and wiped the tears that were now coursing down my cheeks uncontrollably. Sanjay stopped walking, turned to face me, and pulled me to him, holding me as if I were going to break, which I felt I was. He kissed the top of my head, right where the *sindoor* had been drawn, and when he looked at me again his lips were stained with a smidgen of red, which made me smile.

'I'm sorry,' he said. 'I don't want to be angry with you. I suppose if this is the worst that you have done, then I am lucky. Other wives two-time and are lazy. All you want is to make our life better. I don't agree with you, but it is not a bad thing. You are forgiven,' he said. Then, after a pause: 'So let's just forget about it, OK?

'But is there any free weekend in a nice place coming up any time soon?'

'So? How did it go?' Steve asked me a few days later, when I showed up for my session.

'It didn't,' I said. 'Do they give refunds?' I told him what happened, and he nodded sympathetically, thera-pist-style.

'That must make you angry,' he responded, writing on a thick notepad. 'It must have left you terribly sad.'

'It did. Both. But what can I do? This is who he is, and I have to accept it. No sense crying over spilled milk, as my grandmother always says. What's done is done,'

I answered, trying to be cheery. 'Yes, of course I had hoped that something like this would have opened the door to more honesty. That maybe I could have eventually told him about my real job, my real life. But I see that he's not ready for that kind of thing yet. I have to be more patient, give it time. I understand how he is.'

'You're lying to yourself, and you know it,' Steve said softly. 'You know how profoundly unhappy you are. Nobody can help you out of it but yourself.'

'I have to go,' I said, standing up. 'Also, my work schedule is such that it'll be hard for me to come back. Thanks for everything you've done, but I think I'll be OK now.'

I pulled a cheque out of the front pocket of my bag, left it on Steve's desk, and walked out the door.

29

Karishma rang me for days, but I let the calls go to voice-mail and never phoned her back. Shame prevented me from reaching out to her. She sounded so concerned in her messages. And I remembered that look in her eyes when I first told her about the lies I had to tell Sanjay. It was the same look she had the night she first met him, outside Target, when she invited us for *tapas* and he reminded me that we had to go home so I could fry bean sprouts for his sister. I knew she saw me as in a prison of my own making, and not even my glossy job could take that away. Fundamentally, I didn't want to be friends with Karishma any more, because she was right about everything she had seen and sensed of Sanjay. And if she was right about him, then I must have been wrong.

First wedding anniversaries are supposed to be supremely romantic, the one you remember above all others. Sanjay's couple-friends had all talked in superlatives about their own celebrations – the cruises, the Caribbean, the champagne-in-bed breakfasts. They told me how they relived in their memories the exact hour of their wedding.

'This time last year we were about to walk around the fire,' said Shalu, looking over at her husband, Deepak, after she consulted her watch and worked out the time difference. 'Remember, honey? Remember how it rained and rained, but everyone said that was a sign of good luck?'

Our first wedding anniversary was fast approaching, yet not a word was said about it between Sanjay and me, although my mother-in-law did not neglect to remind me that now, after having been married almost twelve months, people would start gossiping about the fact that I had yet to bear a child.

'They will think you are barren,' she said. 'They will think there is something wrong with you. You must conceive.'

Roma, ever the romantic, emailed to ask what we had planned for the big day.

'Flowers in the morning for you, and a sunset walk later, yes?' she asked. 'Perhaps he'll make you pancakes and bring them to you while you lie in bed, with a tiny rose on your tray. I've seen that in the movies.'

I didn't have the heart to tell her that if anyone would be making pancakes, it would be me.

* * *

262

I had read that people in bad marriages flung themselves into their work. I was not that kind of person. Because I felt like a failure as a wife, I didn't see how I could not feel like a failure in front of my computer, or talking to Chris Rock, or sitting around the table at a junket. Around me, everybody else seemed happy and alert, their eyes bright with knowledge and enthusiasm, giggling over the latest pictures of Paris Hilton and P. Diddy. But I couldn't get Kaki out of my head, wondering how, with all the lessons she had taught me about life and karma and being a good girl, I had still managed to mess up something as simple as marriage.

I also had my twenty-fifth birthday to deal with, which was a few weeks before my wedding anniversary. I recalled that how, on every birthday prior to this, I woke up exhilarated, knowing that it would be a special day, even if we did nothing that special to mark it. In my parents' house, Radha, Roma, Ria and I always celebrated together, given that our birthdays were just a few days apart. It was a week when no harsh words were used, when everyone was sweeter and more attentive and less burdened by life. Even Aunt Vimla held back on the criticism. Kaki always sang a three-verse 'Happy Birthday To You' in a mix of Hindi and English that was tuneful and touching, while we four spinster sisters fed one another homemade cake and opened little gifts.

This time last year, I hadn't even met Sanjay.

This year, I would be the only one of our little quartet not present.

30

'TV?' I said to James. 'What do I know about TV?'

James was reading from a memo that Crispin had sent to him about my progress at *Hollywood Insider*. He thought I had learned well here, and now wanted me to try my hand at television. The cable station, focusing on entertainment and celebrities, was off to a good start, and they were looking for producers and researchers. Behind-the-scenes stuff. Detail-driven. Organizing interviews. Writing intros. Timing slots. Coming up with the questions that would make the stars think, or cry, or hopefully both.

'Easy-peasy,' said James, looking relieved that it wasn't a pink slip he was reading from. 'We're billing it around here as a lateral move, but between you and me, it's a promotion. There's even a bit of a raise, although try not to mention that to others, will you? Broadcasting is and always will be the new frontier. People don't have the time or inclination to read four-page features. They

265

want quick, snappy soundbites. Don't you love watching *Entertainment Tonight*? Well, this is going to be just like that, only better. You can do it. What do you think?'

I covered my face with my hands and shook my head. This was, actually, very exciting. I would get to wear an earpiece and stand on the red carpet on Oscars night with a glammed-up anchor person who would look like a celebrity herself, asking the stars what they were wearing and if they thought they'd win. Maybe one day I'd work with Barbara Walters. Maybe one day, when my in-laws were long gone and my husband would finally understand me, I'd even *be* Barbara Walters. I stared at James holding the piece of paper, and the pile of magazines around him and the editorial schedule marked in red on a smooth white board behind his desk. I felt a happiness that was marred only by the fact that my husband these days looked at me with disappointment, his eyes wishing that I could be someone else a bit more to his liking.

'Sure,' I shrugged to James, unthinkingly. 'I'll try TV.'

As I prepared dinner that night, I kept reminding myself how lucky I was. When I had told Deanna about Crispin's offer, she squealed in the way that only she could pull off, and flung her arms around me.

'I sure will miss having you around,' she said, her eyes shining enthusiastically. 'You really are the nicest person here. But people would kill to work in television, so you sure did good.'

I felt fortunate that Crispin had that kind of faith in me. But I couldn't think about it much more, as the carrot *halwa* that I was making for dessert was starting to singe atop the stove.

'*Aarey wah!*' my father-in-law exclaimed later when he saw the spread before him. He and my mother-in-law beamed as they tucked into the steaming platters of food.

Feeling suddenly buoyed by my new position, I had stopped off at the Indian store and picked up special ingredients for tonight's dinner: fresh coriander chutney, fried cashews, sweet yellow rice and Tandoori-style chicken, topped off with an aromatic dessert made from moist and juicy grated carrots and sugar.

Kaki would have been proud.

'Look at all this, Malini,' my mother-in-law said. 'When will you learn to make such good food? See how well trained our Priya is, and you are so useless, sitting all day and painting your nails only.'

I looked over at my sister-in-law, who suddenly stopped chewing and looked at me in humiliation.

'Mummy, that's not really fair,' I said, coming to Malini's defence. 'She's a very talented girl. And you know, she helped me make some of this today, while you were upstairs resting,' I lied.

Malini put down her fork, and left the table, and nobody went after her.

Later, as I did the dishes, Malini came into the kitchen, holding an empty ceramic mug.

'Nice dinner, *bhabi*,' she said. I could tell that she had

been crying. 'You must think you're really smart and special, don't you?' she said, suddenly angry, but squashing her voice. 'Everybody loves your cooking and everybody loves you. Priya this and Priya that. Well, I'm *sick* of it!' she said, tossing a spoon into a soaped-up sink.

'Malini, I'm sorry you are so upset. Your mother didn't mean anything. You know how she can be . . .' I said.

'I know your secret,' Malini spat out, now staring at me straight on.

I lifted my hands out of the warm water, wiped them on my apron, and started to tremble.

'I don't know what you're referring to,' I said, pretending not to care.

'I saw you,' she said. 'It was my friend Tanya's birthday yesterday and we went for lunch to Eurochow and I saw you there. I was upstairs so you didn't see me. You were wearing that cute outfit you had on when we dropped in on you at the office, when you lied about why you were wearing it. You were scribbling things down in a notebook while you were talking to Cameron Diaz. OK, I'm impressed, you were having lunch with one of the Charlie's Angels. I called your office and asked the receptionist about you, and she said you were a reporter. Reporter! But then you came home in your crappy little salwar kameez and started playing little Miss Goody-Two-Shoes . . . you're nothing but a hypocrite,' she said, her cheeks now red with fury. 'I mean, if Mummy and Papa and Sanjay ever found out what you really do, dressing fancy and going here and there, you know they would throw you out of the house. You pretend to be better than me, but you're nothing but a liar and a cheat.'

'Malini, please . . .' I said, my mind a blank. I had no response, but still had to find something to say that would appease her. But my sister-in-law didn't give me the opportunity. She banged a mug down on the counter, and walked out of the kitchen.

'Don't worry,' she said, turning round again at the doorway. 'I won't spill the beans, as long as you start making me look good.'

Sleep, not surprisingly, eluded me that night. Kaki used to tell me to look for what she called 'life's little sign-posts', so I lay in bed as Sanjay slept and tried to figure out what she was referring to.

'They are like little markers on the street,' she said. 'They will guide you to where you need to be.'

Before I started this new job, I was going to have to tell my family the truth.

There was a meeting in a conference room, gathering together the various reporters, researchers and photographers that were about to make the move into the cable television division of the company.

'We'll just discuss what everyone's responsibilities and roles are, go over concerns and questions,' James said, matter-of-factly. 'We want everyone to have as smooth a transition as possible.'

I was told to be there at four, although a phone interview

with Adam Sandler kept me at my desk until a few minutes after that. At least, when I hung up, I had a smile on my face. *He* had sounded bored, but I had been amused. When I looked up, Lynette Dove was standing in front of me, her arms crossed sternly, reminding me of Mrs Pereira from school.

'Yes, Lynette?' I said to her, defying the office decree that she be called 'Ms Dove'. 'Can I help you with something?'

'Just wanted to wish you well in your new cable television endeavours,' she said, now smirking. 'I guess you just weren't cut out for feature writing, were you? It takes skill, you know. Not the kind of thing that anyone off the street can come in and do. At least you learned. You'll no doubt be better off playing maidservant to one of those lacquered-haired silly sorority-sister type presenters they have down there.'

I turned off my computer and stood up.

'I told you when I started this job that you had nothing to worry about with me,' I said, suddenly feeling defiant, but intent on squelching my instinct to slap the woman. 'I told you then that you were the most important person at this magazine, and would continue to be so, long after I'm gone. Well, I'm going, and you are still here. I hope you see now that your insecurities – which are almost psychotic, by the way – were not justified,' I said, pushing past her, my Durga pendant clasped between my fingers.

* * *

At home that night, Sanjay and my in-laws asked me what I wanted to do for my birthday the next day.

'We can go out for dinner,' my mother-in-law suggested. 'No need for you to cook. I have discount coupon from Italian restaurant just opened, very nice. We go there.'

'Thank you, Mummy, that will be fine,' I said.

Dinner was ready and being warmed in the oven awaiting Malini's arrival. According to Sanjay, she had gone to a yoga class and would be home any minute now.

'She must really be enjoying all the *asanas*,' Sanjay said, referring to the poses. 'This is her third class this week, and she does the two-hour ones as well.'

'In the meantime,' my father-in-law instructed me, 'take out the rubbish.'

I wheeled the three big canisters down our driveway and stood there for a second, looking up at the dusky sky. It grew dark by five p.m. these days, when the streets became cold and quiet. I heard tyres screeching around the corner, and looked towards the far end of the street. A white Porsche pulled up a few houses away from ours, and a good-looking black man got out. He came around to the passenger side, opened the door, and out stepped Malini. He slid his arms around her waist and coaxed her towards him, kissing her fully on the lips. I was too shocked even to think about looking away, my mouth open at the passion I saw between my supposedly chaste sister-in-law and a dark-skinned stranger.

271

He saw me first.

And then she did.

I hurried back indoors and went straight into the kitchen, fumbling between casserole dishes and clattering serving spoons. I heard my in-laws welcome Malini home, and her asking them where I was. She came in, her hair windblown, her face frozen from the chilly wind outside and no doubt the fear she felt inside. She stared at me and dropped her shoulder bag to the floor. While she looked afraid, I was the one who was shaking. I loathed confrontations and I could tell that the dormant one that had always stood between us was about to explode.

'I . . . um . . . Malini, don't worry, I won't say anything,' I stammered, nervously twisting a tea towel in my hands.

'Yeah? How the hell do I know that?' she asked, spitting the words out between those perfect, polished teeth. 'What were you doing out there anyway? Were you spying on me?'

'Malini, I was taking out the garbage like I always do at this time. I didn't mean to see you, I promise. What you do with your life is your own business. I'm not going to say anything to mummy-papa or Sanjay. Please, trust me.'

From the next room, my mother-in-law called out to me to start bringing dinner out.

'Yes, Ma, I'm coming,' I said, forcing myself to sound normal. 'Malini and I are just talking about her yoga class.'

I put the tea towel down, and reached out to touch my sister-in-law's arm, to show her that I knew what solidarity in sisterhood meant. After all, I had grown up with three of them.

'Stop smirking,' she said, angrily. 'I'm sick of that look of judgment you have on your face. You always have it. I know what you think of me, that I'm not a good Hindu girl like you. Well, you're not so hot yourself. You think I haven't noticed how unhappy Sanjay has been these past few weeks? He looks pretty fed up with you, too. So don't delude yourself into thinking that you're such a great wife, because you're not.'

Her outburst made me dizzy, and the force of it made me lean up against the tile counter. I was fatigued, filled with despair, and suddenly felt very, very sad.

'You know, I've had just about enough of you,' Malini continued. 'I think it's time for everyone to know the truth about you. Then they'll never believe anything you tell them about me. And maybe you'll be out of the picture soon and I'll be rid of you and your superior attitude forever. So I'm going to go out there right now and tell them everything,' she threatened.

I was too tired to speak. Malini and I had never been close, but I had no idea she hated me so. Every conflict eventually takes on a life of its own, and that was where we were with this one. I looked at Malini, and was vaguely reminded of a saying I had learnt from Mrs Pereira, something about cowards being those who should be feared the most. Malini was going to divulge

273

all about me before I could do the same about her – a pre-emptive strike if ever there was one.

This was definitely one of Kaki's little signposts.

'Don't trouble yourself,' I said to her, turning and walking out of the kitchen. 'I'll do it for you.'

My spirit was too flattened to offer details and explanations. So I simply said: 'I am not a receptionist. I am a magazine journalist. And I am quite well-regarded, too. I go all over town. I wear Western clothes from fancy shops. I have been lying to you all this time. I am not who you think I am, but have become who I always wanted to be.'

As I said the words, I realized how bitter I was, how angry. I wanted to go upstairs to my room, shut the door, and leave my in-laws to fetch their own food for once. They sat in silence, barely blinking. Without waiting for a response from anyone, I took off my apron, and bowed down to my mother-in-law and father-in-law in my usual goodnight ritual. They didn't even move.

When I awoke the next morning, I initially forgot it was my birthday. I stayed in my room for a while, gazing out the window, thinking but not really thinking. Just processing, really, as they say in LA, letting the thoughts come to me without sorting them out. Sanjay, who had spent the night in the guest room, came in and asked me to go downstairs.

'We need to talk about this as a family,' he said, in a rare nod to open communication. We can't all just go on as if nothing has happened.'

The five of us gathered in the living room. My father-in-law was the first to speak.

'By the way, happy birthday,' he said gruffly. I thought of my three sisters around the birthday cake, Kaki singing, and everyone feeding one another afterwards. Those were the sweetest birthday celebrations ever.

'Now, Priya, this is a most serious situation,' he said. 'You have defied us. You have been doing God-knows-what with God-knows-whom, behind our backs this whole time. No good girl is brought up to be a liar,' he said, as I glanced over at Malini, whose body tightened in fear.

'Do you have anything to say, or will you keep sitting quietly, like an innocent?' he asked, his face stern and his voice steady.

'Papa,' I began. 'I'm very, very sorry that I have hurt and disobeyed you all like this,' I said, truthfully. 'It was never my intention. It just happened.'

They listened in silence as I told them about a woebegone Shanisse calling me to fill in for her, about a drunken Rex Hauser, and then a contrite one hours later. I told them about Crispin's offer, and how I couldn't turn it down, and the clothes, and the luncheons, and the stars who had become my friends. They listened without expression – although Malini's face alternated between jealousy and regret – when I told them that Arabella

Tomas and I met for lunch every few months in a Brentwood café and talked about our lives, and that Maia Mourtos had sent me birthday flowers yesterday, and that Rex Hauser *always* asked about me. And then I told them about the new job offer, and how I had decided to take it.

'It has been a good life,' I said, implicitly acknowledging that I was ready to let it go, even if I wasn't. 'It has served me well. I seek your forgiveness for not telling you, but you would never have allowed me to pursue it. So I kept it quiet. But as you can see, it has never interfered with my life here. I would like to think that I remain the daughter-in-law that you wanted me to be.'

Sanjay looked, for the first time, almost chastened.

'Still, you lied,' he said, spitting the words out like a five-year-old in a school playground. 'Again. I feel like I don't even know who you are.'

'That is something I wanted us to remedy,' I said to him quietly.

'What has been your salary?' my mother-in-law asked, finally saying something.

'Fifty-five thousand,' I told them, refusing to lie any more. 'But with this new TV job, probably a little more.'

Sanjay looked furious again, realizing that I made more than he did.

'Where is that money?' my father-in-law asked.

'I opened a savings account. It is all there. I was thinking, maybe a few years from now, that I would buy you something nice, anything you wanted.'

276

Silence again, as they sat and simmered in a mix of what looked like envy, astonishment and confusion about what to do with me next.

'Wah wah! Movie stars and making so much money!' my mother-in-law said, suddenly smiling large and looking excited. 'That is very good pay. We can do with it. Malini has to get married still. And it's very nice, we can tell our friends that see, our Priya has got such a fancy job, not like their boring shopkeepers and all,' she announced. 'You should not have lied, but now that it's done, it's done. *Bas*, you continue. We forgive you. Maybe you are not such a dumb girl after all.'

Sanjay, as always, nodded in agreement with his mother, while my father-in-law said nothing. Malini got up and left the room. I went after her, this time unafraid. I grabbed her by the arm and forced her to look at me.

'I would *never* have told them about you,' I said. 'Your life is your business. I wish you had trusted me. And I wish I could have been able to trust you. We are almost sisters, after all.'

Malini shrugged her arm free, and went upstairs.

The birthday call from Delhi came later that evening.

'Is Sanjay taking you out for your first birthday together?' my mother asked, all excited.

'No, we're tired. Had a busy day,' I said, stifling the tears. After all the drama of the day, nobody felt much like going out.

'Our heartiest wishes for your birthday, darling,' my mother said. 'We miss you so very much here, but thank the Lord for your happiness.'

'Now what's your problem?' Sanjay asked later, as I folded down the bedcovers. 'What's with the sad face? It's all over. We forgive you. In fact, I think my parents have a new respect for you. So it's all worked out for the best. You may carry on there if you wish,' he said, changing into his pyjamas as I slammed the cupboard doors shut. I was so angry I could barely breathe. I should have been happy, and relieved, that it was all now out in the open. But something about their attitude, all of them, left me sick with rage.

Karishma was thrilled to hear from me the next day.

'I've been so worried about you,' she said. 'Steve said you'd stopped going to see him, and then you didn't call me back. It was beginning to freak me out.'

'I'm fine,' I said. 'Actually, I'm not fine. They found out.'

I told her what happened, and she first gave me some platitude about how it was all for the best.

'But here's what concerns me,' she said, tuning in to my sorrow. 'It's like they never respected you. It's only now that you have an important job with lots of money, they are suddenly happy to have you around. What would they do if you said you didn't want to work there any more? Kick you out of the house?'

Karishma, as always, had nailed it. She had asked the right questions, the kind of questions I should have asked Sanjay who, clueless as he was, would probably not have been able to answer them.

31

Kaki didn't faint when she saw me. Instead, she put her arms round me and cried, although I knew they were tears for her, and not for me.

'This time last year you were preparing for your wedding,' she said, looking at her watch. 'Now, a year later, you are back with us. My smallest dove has returned.'

I had always thought that people who left marriages did so casually and cavalierly, as if it involved no more fore-thought than driving to Burger King on a Friday night. In between my birthday and two days before my first wedding anniversary, when I boarded a Delhi-bound flight at Los Angeles Airport, thoughts of my becoming a divorcee never left my head. I would forever carry the stain of failure, of the inability to compromise, of not knowing how to keep the peace in a Hindu household. I knew that everyone would tut-tut upon my return, that not only were there once four spinster sisters, but see, now one has returned from her marriage, besmirched and sullied. Where the others were untouched, I had become untouchable.

I used to hear people talk about me, when they thought I was safely out of earshot.

'See, after only *one year* she has come back,' they would say, as if it would have been more acceptable if I had stuck it out for three years, or five, or ten.

At least my parents didn't hold it against me. And Radha and Roma and Ria were as sweet and supportive as ever, although Roma told me sadly that, until me, she had never even talked to a divorced person before. And Ria said there should be some law against what my husband and in-laws had done to me, gradually eroding my spirit and causing tiny fissures in my heart I was sure would never heal. My sisters didn't, I know, quite get why I had to leave, but trusted that I needed to.

'They kept whatever jewellery you gave me, Mummy,' I told her sadly. 'When I first got there, they got me a safe in the bank, but didn't let me put my name on it. I was stupid, and agreed. When I left, they kept it all. But I didn't care to fight for it. I'm sorry.'

'Don't be sorry, darling,' my mother soothed. 'Gold comes and goes, but a daughter is a daughter. You are here with us now. We will never send you where you are not wanted and welcomed. Such a shame though. That Sanjay is such a handsome boy.'

* * *

I thought of him all the time.

He hadn't even asked me to stay.

Leaving was the easy part. Knowing that my presence never mattered that much – that's what destroyed me.

The people at work seemed to be the only ones who wanted me to stay. 'I don't understand it,' Crispin said, clearly confused, when I went in to pick up my things and my last paycheck. 'So your marriage fell apart? So what? That happens here all the time. It doesn't mean you have to go anywhere. You have a job and you earn a nice living, and you'll be perfectly fine without a husband. Why do you want to return to India?'

'Believe me, I have thought of that,' I replied. 'But I don't know how to live here,' I said, now softly crying, as Crispin still looked perplexed. 'I don't know how to do the things that need to be done. I don't know how to fill in those tax forms, I never knew what a mortgage was until I came here. I never had to know about refinancing and IRAs and smog tests. Sanjay protected me from these things. The country is too big and the people too foreign and I don't know how to be alone here.'

Crispin got up from his chair and came around his desk to where I was sitting and sobbing.

'You'll learn,' he said gently. 'Your friends will help you, and you'll learn. We are here for you as well,' he said, laying a hand on my shoulder.

'It's too hard,' I said, gathering myself. 'You have been so tremendously kind, and I thank you for all your goodwill. But everything hurts, and I just want to be with my parents.'

'If that's your decision . . .' Crispin said, tentatively hugging me. 'But if you change your mind, you'll always have a place here with us.'

Downstairs, Deanna was putting my things in a box for me.

'I think you're making a big mistake,' she said, her voice quaking. 'I don't want you to leave, and I don't think you should leave. This was your dream job, remember?'

She handed me a card that she said had just arrived, and I immediately recognized the handwriting on the envelope.

'My dear Priya,' Maia Mourtos had written. 'How sorry I was to learn of the collapse of your marriage, and your decision to return to India. But I would be the last person to tell you to ignore what is in your heart. I know that when love is lost, it seems like everything is. But we are stronger than we think we are. I hope we will continue to be friends. My best wishes are with you.'

Sanjay saw me pack my bags, shrugged his shoulders, and went back downstairs to his parents. My mother-in-law cried, but only because she now had to go through the added expense and inconvenience of finding another wife for her son. Malini was in her room, the door shut, and my father-in-law kept his face hidden behind his newspaper.

Karishma was waiting for me in her car outside. As I got in, I saw Sanjay standing by the window, staring out at me. I saw him mouth something to his mother, something that looked like an appeal of some sort. She must not have responded to him, because as Karishma backed out of the driveway, Sanjay let the curtain drop.

32

The children in the neighbourhood who, during our wedding week, had sung that silly little ditty about Sanjay and I, sitting in a tree, K-I-S-S-I-N-G, were now quiet. They pointed, or they cast their eyes downward on to the *paan*-stained pavement. They had heard about me. Before I had even landed, Sanjay's mother had called all her friends in Delhi and told them that I had been a terrible daughter-in-law, and had been asked to leave. She said that I lied (true), and stole (false) and was lazy (false) and had too much of my own mind (true, apparently).

'She called you a worthless wife,' Aunt Vimla said, when she stopped by to pay her condolences upon the death of my marriage. 'Maybe you became too American there. I told you, remember? Obey, be quiet, and you will always be happy. But you didn't listen.' She stopped talking when my sisters entered the room to cluster around me protectively.

***

I lost fifteen pounds the first month I was back. I would wake up in the middle of the night, dazed, unsure where I was in the darkness of my room. I put my hand out next to me to feel Sanjay's back, like I had always done, and instead felt a lumpy pillow. I listened for his soft snores, and heard only the crickets outside, and the occasional ring of a bicycle bell in the night.

Vivacious! was still arriving, around the same time every month, between the fourteenth and the seventeenth, depending on whether the postman was having a good week or not. I read it now with detachment, no longer caught up in the frothy words on the page about the unreal lives of people on the big screen. I considered maybe applying there for a job. No woman in my family had ever worked. But no woman in my family had ever left her husband either.

Any day now, I thought, I would hear the news about Sanjay and a new wife. Technically, he and I weren't even divorced yet. Thanks to the creakingly slow workings of the Indo-US legal system, it would take some time before he and I would make our separation official. But that would be no impediment for any other sweet and soft-headed girl who might eventually fall for Sanjay's good looks and the promises of abundance that are suggested by the idea of life in America. A religious Hindu wedding would suffice, a walk around the fire being as binding as an appearance before a judge at City Hall. It was only a matter of time before Sanjay moved on with his life, while I had gone backwards in mine.

After I'd been back two months, my father stopped hiding in shame. He began to go out again, hopeful that his friends wouldn't ask him too many questions. My mother was stoic, responding to queries about me both polite and abrasive with a non-committal: 'What can you do? Everything happens for a reason.' Kaki put away her statue of the doves, and tripled the numbers of dried chilies hanging outside her front door which she was convinced would help to divert the evil eye that she said was being cast upon us as a family.

That, or something, worked.

Radha arose at 3.11 a.m. one night, and pattered quietly into my parents' bedroom, stirring me from sleep as she went. I stood in the doorway as she sat on my parents' bed and started to cry.

'What is it, beti?' my mother asked, her voice thick with fear. 'Has something happened in the house?'

'He's back,' Radha sobbed. 'Nishant. He came to me just now. He said he was back to be with me.'

'It was just a bad dream,' my father said, rolling over to sleep. 'Too many movies you've been watching.'

As Radha returned to her room, I took her hand and said to her: 'I believe you.'

Two days later, my mother came home from the market looking pale and flustered. Once inside the house, she leaned against the front door, breathless.

'You won't believe who I saw on the street,' she said to the four of us, gathered around a small coffee table playing Monopoly.

'Asha. Nishant's mother.'

Radha dropped the small bundle of paper money she was holding, and let it be scattered away by the fan that whirled languorously overhead. Our family had not seen Nishant's family since his funeral, eleven years ago. After his death, they had all relocated to London, all of us so crushed with a sadness that had weakened our ability and theirs to reach out to one another. I knew, deep down, that my mother blamed Nishant for drinking, driving and then dying, and that Nishant's mother bitterly begrudged Radha for being the last person to have seen her son alive.

'What did she say, Mummy?' I asked timorously, the only one to speak.

'They're back from London, just for a few months. They want to come here and see you Radha, just to say hello. I think we should welcome them.'

* * *

290

We four sisters fried and baked and sautéed the entire morning, preparing for tea. Radha was there, but not, keeping the shells and throwing away the peas, and almost slicing off her finger as she peeled spongy eggplants.

'Eleven years is a long time to not see people who were almost my family,' she said, crying as much from the squirts of onion juice as from the memories of a love long lost. 'I feel sick with nerves about it.'

They arrived at exactly four p.m., Nishant's parents filling the doorway. They smiled half-heartedly, sharing our nervousness. As they stepped over the threshold, they parted to reveal someone standing behind them, at first glimpse of whom we all gasped, convinced that Nishant had returned from the pyre.

It was Nayan, his younger brother, now all grown up like the rest of us.

Tea turned into dinner, so we were glad to have prepared enough food to feed a Rajasthani army. Afterwards, my mother and Nishant's mother hugged like sisters, and cried like they did the night he died. My father turned to Nishant's father and said: 'I have no sons, but I know the loss of a child is God's cruellest curse. My heart is with you.'

Radha and Nayan had stared at one another through the various courses of *bhel puri* and *dahi wada* and *channa masala*. I had seen Roma also gazing at Nayan, at his poise and his perfect features. I know she remembered that Kaki had wanted Nayan for her, had Nishant lived. But as Roma stood next to Nayan, she had to bend down so he could help himself to a dollop of chutney, and I knew then and there it would never happen.

But as Nayan and Radha said goodbye, he reached over and lightly touched her hand.

'I know you loved my brother like I did,' he said, not taking his eyes off hers. 'And I know how much he loved you. Even without him, I am trying my best to become the man he was.'

Later, as my mother put away the good dishes, she said to me: 'Did you see them together? It's like Radha has found the other half of her soul in Nayan.'

They were engaged two weeks later.

It went off without a hitch. In a nod to superstition, Kaki had decreed that no alcohol be consumed the night before the wedding. When we returned home from the Imperial Hotel where Radha and Nayan's nuptials had taken place, my grandmother let out a mighty sigh that now, perhaps, the curse upon us girls had finally been lifted. She brought out her statue again, and petted the biggest dove.

'My Radha is going to a new life in London,' she said through tears. 'Now the heavens will open for the rest of you. Even you, Priya. Even you will find someone again.'

My father took off his Bally shoes, wrapped them carefully in their original box and shook his head.

Three weeks after Radha and Nayan left for their exotic honeymoon – where I got Naina Tal, she got New

Zealand – my father received a call from a distant cousin in San Jose. The cousin, Uncle Vishnu, had been to a conference in San Francisco and had been rather impressed by a young man who stood up to talk about the latest innovations in motherboard circuitry.

'The boy didn't even have to stand on a podium,' my father told us excitedly later. 'He managed to reach the microphone, just like that. Vishnu says he is at least six-foot three. He has made enquiries, and the boy is single and good looking. Truly, maybe, the Gods are smiling upon you all this year.'

Photos of six-footer Suraj and a swooning Roma were exchanged, and the dance began.

The night was quiet and rainy, with only Ria and I at home. My parents had escorted Roma to meet with Suraj, who had just flown in that morning from San Francisco. Unlike what had happened with me, they were not going to wait until an engagement ceremony to meet. They had talked on the phone numerous times, exchanged happy and thoughtful emails, and had decided not to commit until they went out together, alone, at least three times. Kaki had initially resisted such an approach as 'too modern', but when my mother reminded her where hard-core tradition had got me, Kaki relented, hoping that perhaps Roma may now have won the biggest prize of all. Ria and I were not allowed to go along, the fear among parents being that an eligible boy earmarked for a particular girl might opt for one of her sisters instead, his height notwithstanding.

Ria was looking for old clothes to donate to the shelter where she worked, while I was huddled beneath the coarse pink blanket that Kaki had knitted forty years ago, half-watching television. A local network was broadcasting some Oscar coverage from the previous night. Wide-angled shots across the red carpet took in clipboard-carrying, earpiece-wearing television staff, clustered in mini-conferences around their star anchors – Matt Lauer, Nancy O'Dell, Joan Rivers.

I should have been there, I thought to myself. I *could* have been there. Had I not hitched up my petticoat and fled, I would have been there.

I stared out into the black night, the only light provided by a streetlamp that flickered on and off. Jagdish's dry goods store was barricaded with steel shutters, now shiny and noisy with rain. It was the kind of night I used to see in my dreams, the night that I had dreaded.

The street was empty and quiet, with only a pair of headlights passing through every so often, on their way somewhere. A taxi pulled up a few doorways down, and someone got out, paid the driver, pulled a suitcase out of the trunk, and started walking in the rain towards our house.

He stopped right outside the window and looked in, the light from our living room casting itself out.

I recognized the orange windcheater immediately.

I don't know why I did, but I ran to the door, knocking over a brass jug and the umbrella stand as I went.

Sanjay stood in the doorway, his face wet with rain and tears. 'Hi,' he said, as expressive as ever.

I reached out and pulled him out of the rain, but let him stand in the hallway.

'Sanjay, what are you doing here?' I asked, my mind cloudy with confusion, the drip-drip of raindrops from his jacket onto the floor the only thing that seemed real.

'I didn't want to be without you. I came back for you,' he said, putting his suitcase down. 'Let's go home.'

'Sanjay, you have some nerve . . .' I was angry – that he had waited three months before realizing this, and that he assumed I would fall at his feet in delight and relief.

Ria came downstairs when she heard Sanjay's voice, disbelief on her face.

'Oh, look what the rains have brought,' she said, sarcasm creeping into her voice. 'All sorts of debris gets washed up at this time of year.'

'Ria, it's OK,' I said. 'I can handle this.'

Just then, the front door opened again, and in walked Roma, my parents and Kaki. The happiness on their faces – evidently the meeting with Suraj had gone well – suddenly turned to astonishment. They all stood there, stunned, as Sanjay bent over and touched the feet of everyone but Roma, whom he nodded at instead. Roma instantly looked thrilled again, as if the happy ending she had always wanted for me was now right before her.

'What brings you here?' Kaki asked Sanjay, her arms folded in front of her, her hair looking more grey beneath the light overhead.

'I came back for Priya,' he said. 'I didn't want to be without her any more.'

'What? Do you think she's just been sitting here all these weeks, doing nothing?' she asked, sternly.

'Actually, she *has* just been sitting doing nothing,' Roma said, still smiling.

'*Chup!*' Kaki said, instructing Roma to be quiet.

'Don't let me be without her,' Sanjay said to Kaki, now finally realizing that she ran this family. 'I go out with all my friends, and it's just me and all of them in twos. I hate it.'

'So that's it?' I asked, my voice rising. 'You want me back because you need a partner on Saturday nights?'

'No, no, Priya,' he said, shaking his head. 'You misunderstand me. I'm stupid. I don't know how to say what I really feel sometimes.'

'Look what I have,' Sanjay said, reaching into his pocket. He pulled out a key, attached by a chain to a large silver 'P'. 'I got us our own house. That's why it took me so long to come here for you. I wanted everything to be perfect. It will be just you and me, no interference. Work, don't work, I don't care. Please, come home with me.'

Kaki spoke up again. 'You think that you can come back here, dangling a keychain, and our Priya will jump like a Jack-in-the-box? Well, my son, you are quite wrong. We want all our girls to be married, but not miserable.'

My father, who had asked me little about the collapse of my marriage, finally spoke.

'Sanjay, if you really want my daughter, you will have to prove that you are deserving of her. Priya,' he said, turning to me, 'I never apologized for sending you there, when my instincts told me what kind of people they were. I am willing to give this boy a second chance, but only if you want me to.'

I teared up at my father's confession and wanted to hug him, but such things were not done in my family. All eyes were on me as I decided what to do. Sanjay gave me the keychain, and I let the warm wetness of the 'P' soak into my palm.

'Do you want some hot *pista* milk?' I asked him, unable to think beyond beverages.

'No, I just want you to come home with me,' Sanjay said softly.

'You know, Sanjay, I thought you would protect me,' I said to him, not caring that everyone was listening. 'You were to protect me from those who didn't cherish me the way they were supposed to. You were meant to love me enough.'

We both knew we were talking about his family. But still, after all this time, and despite my status as a near-divorcee, I couldn't bring myself to complain about them to him. Kaki used to tell me that speaking ill of one's in-laws in public would rate a return in a future life as a gnat.

Shrouded in his orange jacket, Sanjay suddenly looked shrunken and small, and I felt sorry for him. Apparently, Kaki picked up on that, and led him by his hand to the sofa, like he was a child about to be disciplined.

'Come, sit,' she said, easing him down. 'Sanjay, are you aware of the vows that you took the night you got married? I know, it was all in Sanskrit, and you young people think yourselves too modern to understand such things. But now, maybe too late, let me tell you.' She closed her eyes, put her hands atop Sanjay's, and started to sing the ancient hymn that is recited by priests as Hindu couples walk seven times around the fire.

'One is for vigour,' she began to chant, in English now. 'Two for vitality. Three for prosperity and four for happiness. Five is for cattle and six for the seasons. Seven is for friendship. And then, you and Priya looked at one another and said: "To me, be devoted." She was devoted to you and your family, but can you say the same, Sanjay? Until you can, there is no reason under God's sky why our youngest dove should fly off with you again.'

Sanjay looked contrite, his eyes on the floor.

'It is late,' Kaki said. 'You will come home with me. You may stay for as long as you like, until you and Priya decide what you want. When we first gave her to you, we gave her too easily. Now, you must work for her. You must woo her,' my grandmother said, reaching out and touching my hand. 'You must show us that you love her enough.'

As I was making *masala* omelettes for breakfast the next morning, Sanjay was at the door.

'Let's go do something fun,' he said, as I spotted a taxi waiting behind him.

Twenty minutes later, we boarded a rickshaw and meandered through Chandni Chowk, the old silver market that was now a frenetically bustling bazaar selling everything from beaded belts to cotton bed sheets. We stopped for *pani puri* from a man on a bicycle, and giggled as we haggled over five rupees for a skinny chiffon scarf that Sanjay wanted for his secretary. We talked about the weather, and jetlag, and what new restaurants had opened in Northridge. I wanted him to say something of more depth and significance, but wasn't about to ask him to.

Later, as the rains looked like they were about to start up again, Sanjay and I stopped for *idli sambar* at a small canteen. We took a booth at the back, and waited while a man in a stained vest with a towel thrown over his shoulder took our order.

'In California, this place would have been shut down long ago,' Sanjay laughed, as the man returned with a metal jug of water which he slammed down atop the Formica-covered table.

'How is your family?' I asked, not being able to rein in my curiosity any more.

'They're OK,' he said, shrugging his shoulders. 'They were a bit pissed when you left, and then when I got my own place. But I don't really care what they say any more. You know, Priya, I went to see that guy Steve, your friend's husband.'

I gasped in astonishment, finding it hard to imagine Sanjay reclining on Steve's black leather couch.

'He's good,' he said. 'I can't believe what a knucklehead I've been. He made me see what I was doing wrong, and why I was so obsessed with pleasing my parents. I've worked through some of those issues.' I smiled at how Sanjay had picked up Steve's lingo.

'And Malini? How is she?' I asked, tentatively.

'Geez, that sister of mine. Man, she had a whole load of issues. We found out she was sneaking around behind our backs, dating some guy. Papa flipped, of course. They sent her off to a convent school in Simla,' he said, shaking his head. 'We figured she couldn't misbehave that much in some Indian outpost.'

'That seems a bit extreme, no?' I asked, now feeling sorry for my sister-in-law.

'Yeah. I guess they'll let her come home again soon. Just wanted to teach her a lesson. I think they're hoping they'll just marry her off, problem solved.'

'But it isn't, is it?' I said, quietly, dousing one of my soft, spongy *idlis* with the spicy *sambar*. 'Marriage doesn't solve problems, does it? It just creates new ones.'

As the drizzle outside slowly turned harder and faster, this felt like the first time that Sanjay and I were having a truly honest conversation.

'I wasn't a very good husband, was I?' he said. 'A bit of a bonehead, I know. But I've read a few books, watched Oprah. I think I know how to be better at it.'

I smiled, took his hand, and we went home.

Two weeks later, Kaki dropped Sanjay off at my house as she went off to do the marketing. She was beaming as she went, no doubt thinking about Roma's engagement party next week and praying hopefully for my own reunion with Sanjay. We had spent most of the past fortnight together, acting like a newly-courting couple instead of one that had been married a year but hadn't even celebrated a first anniversary. I loved him still, had never really stopped. Now, I was ready to go back to him.

He was clutching a fistful of wilted roses.

'Sorry, this was all they had,' he said, staring at the drooping buds. 'But they in no way reflect my abiding love for you. Please, Priya, come home with me,' he said. 'I promise you, we'll make a happy new life together.'

His face was as handsome as ever, his smile winsome and full. I wanted to kiss him. His ring had never left my finger, but now, I really wanted it to mean something again. The flowers looked bountiful and rich. I told him that yes, I wanted to be his wife again.

'Great!' he said, smiling broadly. 'And listen, Priya, if you want to work, that's fine,' he said. 'I'll let you.'

Everything stopped, the roses withered. Those words pinged around in my brain. He'll *let* me. He'll *let* me.

'You just don't get it, do you Sanjay?' I asked, sad again and standing back from him. 'You don't understand what I need, or what really went wrong between us. You think that a key on a silver 'P' will fix the flaws in our union, but I'm sorry, it's not enough. We are husband and wife, Sanjay. Husbands and wives don't need to get one another's permission for anything, at least not in the marriage that I want to have. Do you understand that, at least?'

Sanjay put the flowers down on a table, and shook his head.

'I'm so clueless,' he said. 'Things don't come out of my mouth the way they're supposed to. I mean well, Priya. See that at least. Steve said I had to learn to be conversant in the language of my heart, because my head is a bit thick sometimes.'

He looked up at me again, earnestly. 'Kaki told me that one of the wedding vows meant: "In my word, you rejoice with all your heart." Priya, I promise you that from now on, I will rejoice in *your* word with all my heart. We are equals. Actually, you are better than me.

'Plus, you know, Hollywood is waiting for you,' he said, laughing through tears.

Sanjay folded his hands together, bent down and touched my feet.

'Please forgive me,' he said, as I lifted him up by his shoulders, embarrassed and yet so moved that I couldn't speak. Nobody had ever touched my feet before.

'Please just know that any time you feel unwanted in the world, and by anybody in it, that you are wanted in my world.'

Ria came out of her room and was peering over the railings, and the look of disdain that constantly lingered on her face disappeared.

Instead, she smiled, looked at me, and nodded in approval so slightly that only a sister could pick it up.

Aunt Vimla wanted to know if I would get my jewellery back, while my mother nudged her in her fleshy stomach to keep her quiet. Kaki put one hand on my head, and one on Sanjay's, and placed them together gently, as she had done on our wedding day.

'In America I understand people live together before they get married, to see if it will work. Consider your past year that. Now, today, you *are* married,' she said. 'Never hold an ill thought for anyone, and all the world's riches will be yours.'

As we left my family's house to fly back to Los Angeles, the neighbourhood children gathered around again, singing their song. 'Sanjay and Priya sitting in a tree, K-I-S-S-I-N-G, first comes love, then comes marriage . . .'

And, just as they predicted, by the time the next Oscars rolled around, there was a baby in a golden carriage.